URUS

URUS

Bob Grant

To order additional copies of this book, contact:
Xlibris Corporation
1-888-795-4274
www.Xlibris.com
Orders@Xlibris.com
47333

CONTENTS

Dedication

The four people who gave me the inspiration and confidence to write this book are: The person who gave me the idea to write a story was Violet Sauers. She is a very sharp 90+ year old person I have known for my entire life. Violet and her family have been more like relatives than friends. The second person is Glen Uhlenkott, he is the first friend I met in Moses Lake almost half a century ago. He read the first draft of URUS and sent back corrections that took me over a day to implement. The third person is Peggy Majors. She read the story when it was in about its fourth draft and raved about it so much I felt it may be good enough to publish. The fourth person who needs mentioning is my cousin Charles Olson. He is a retired Seattle Pacific University professor who spent many hours finding errors in what I thought was my final draft. If not for these people, this book would have never been completed.

Chapter 1

The Disc

The year was 1971, the time was 2:35 a.m., the place was Old Pacific Coast Highway between San Clemente and Oceanside, California. I was driving an old 1952 Studebaker Commander V8 Starliner (It was a hot car that could slip down the highway like you were floating on a cloud but take a corner too sharp and you would scrape your elbow on the pavement . . . but at least it didn't have the bullet-nose any more. People would tell me, "You drive a Studebaker? I can't tell if it's coming or going." I would answer, "Just look out your window as I pass by, then you should be able to figure it out."

My story starts as I was returning to San Diego from a weekend in Santa Barbara where I attended a buddy's wedding. He had just graduated from a teacher's college and was exchanging marriage vows with a lovely girl who lived next door to my parent's house. Most of his other guests were well on their way to careers. I, on the other hand, had spent four years in the military, had recently found a job in Southern California and was feeling a little melancholy as my headlights cut through the clear blackness of a California night.

There was a lot to think about as I guided my car down that lonely stretch of highway. I was thinking about my future and how uninspired I was when out of the night sky, those thoughts were blown away. Out of the starlit blackness, a bright light appeared to be moving closer and growing larger. At first I thought it was an airplane trying to land on the highway but as I watched the object get closer, it settled as soft and quiet as a feather in a field not far from Highway 101. I pulled over and stopped the old Studebaker to witness the lights become stationary, then fade into the night for a few minutes before they grew brighter just before shooting into the air like a flaming arrow and becoming another fiery point of light in the heavens.

Sitting there with my heart pounding, I was about to start the car when a few hundred yards ahead; a pair of brake lights blinked on only to fade away as the car left the scene. Quickly I drove to the spot I figured the mysterious car had occupied, stopped again, retrieved a flashlight from the glove compartment and walked to the side of the road.

My heart was now pounding in my throat as I entered the field that had just been occupied by a UFO. The light from the flashlight swished back and forth in front of me as I carefully placed my feet between the rocks and bushes. I had traveled less than thirty yards when my light caught a shiny object leaning on a small rock. Picking it up, it resembled a shinny silver dollar. Except this disc-shaped piece of metal was not much thicker than a strand of hair and couldn't be bent, scratched or broken. The small hole in its center made me think it was some kind of recording device. My first instinct was to take it to the authorities but soon realized if I did that, I would probably never see it again. Then I thought maybe if I let the media have it they would be able to find out what it was. I disregarded that notion because other people I know who have volunteered information to the press were always criticized as being crack-pots or worse. The safest course was to figure out what this strange disc was by myself. All of a sudden the thought occurred to me that they might discover this disc is missing and streak back here to find it. My feet started moving and the distance between me and my Studebaker melted away like a snowflake touching my tongue. In a flash I jumped behind the wheel of the Starliner, smoked the tires, and made a hasty exit toward home.

The next morning, I tried to enlarge pictures of it to see if it had grooves like a 45 or 78 rpm record. Either I couldn't enlarge them enough or there weren't any. Next I tried modifying an old phonograph turntable by inserting a new professional grade diamond-tipped needle in the arm before attempting to play it. No matter how fast or slow the turntable spun, the only sound I could hear was the needle sliding back and forth. After removing the disc it was apparent not even the diamond-tipped needle could scratch the artifact. Nothing seemed to unlock the secret I felt the disc was keeping locked inside.

A couple weeks of frustration went by. My failure to open it led me to return to the site where the disc was found. This time I brought a rented metal detector to give myself a better chance of finding a device that would make it possible to read the information on the disc.

The rocky field was empty except for the indentations of the three evenly spaced pods of the craft's landing gear. Figuring the focal point of those three pods was a good place to start, I soon became engrossed with watching the meter on the metal detector as each of the concentric search patterns was completed. I didn't notice a shabbily dressed elderly man approach my search. When he tapped me on the shoulder I almost jumped out of my skin. He apologized and asked what I was doing out there. Since it was really none of his business I replied a little sarcastically, "Looking for my money clip."

He reached out and grabbed my arm, looked me in the eye and said, "The government has been out here for weeks and has covered this area with a fine-toothed comb and has found nothing. I'll ask you again."

Before he could finish, I jerked my arm from his grasp and told him it was none of his business. He took a step backwards and then said something odd, "And why are you looking here for your silver dollar money clip?"

That got my attention because I know I hadn't mentioned anything about the size or shape of the money clip. The hobo looking old man exited the area only to lean up against a tree at the far edge of the field.

It was starting to get dark by the time my search terminated; suddenly the mysterious hobo reappeared standing at my side. This time he was more forceful when he said, "I know what you are looking for and maybe I can help you, but you have to be honest with me and tell me the truth."

There was no way I was going to confide in this stranger so I told him to leave me alone. He did and I thought that was the end of it but his words "I know what you are looking for . . ." kept me from having a good night's sleep for weeks.

As time passed, my desire to discover the true importance of the find waned until one day when I entered my apartment. I noticed an opaque square-based pyramid about four inches tall on my desk. Nothing in the apartment was disturbed or missing, even the door and windows were still locked. As soon as I picked the pyramid up, an interior soft yellowish light began to get brighter and brighter until it was pure white. There was no heat and the light stayed inside the object. I was about to put it down when words began to appear on the triangular face of the pyramid. In a few seconds a message appeared, "Insert key here" and a hairline crack formed near the base. I was confused; I didn't own a key that small. I set the pyramid down again and the light went out so I picked it up again and sure enough the light came on again. It took me a few minutes to realize that maybe the thin disc found over a month ago was in fact a key. I reached into my back pocket, pulled out my wallet and found the "key" between some photographs.

My heart started beating faster and I could feel excitement flowing through my whole body. It seemed an eternity before I extracted that metallic wafer and with trembling fingers, held it centimeters from the base of the pyramid. Thoughts were racing through my brain as to reasons I should or shouldn't slip that key into the slot. The course of action I finally decided to take was to set up my Super 8 camera on the shelf behind my desk and set it on "record" to be able to see what would happen after the wafer was inserted. With that settled, I slipped the key into the slot as I replaced it on the desk. No sooner was the key completely inserted than a holographic page of symbols and diagrams appeared to be suspended in air a foot or so from the pyramid. I had no idea what I was looking at but that didn't matter long because standing in my room was the old man from the sighting field,.

He began to walk toward the desk and said, "Thank you for returning our key".

I told him to stop. Ignoring me, he continued walking toward the desk. Holding out my outstretched arm, I jumped between him and the desk and insisted he stop! He stopped less than a foot from my extended hand and replied, "I am not here to injure you, just to collect the key." Before I could blink, he had interlocked his fingers with mine and had twisted my arm to force me on my tiptoes. With this advantage he moved me around like a puppet on a stick. Picking up the projection device, he released me and turned toward the door.

I couldn't just let him walk out of the room so I blurted our, "Before you go, tell me who you work for."

"I don't work for anyone" he replied, "You just don't understand what you found, do you?"

Trying to regain a little dignity I responded, "No, why don't you tell me?"

The old man stopped in his tracks, turned and looked at me again with a solemn expression and just stared for an inordinate length of time. I froze with the realization that I could be in mortal danger now since he didn't need me anymore. He had already recovered the disc and pyramid. To my astonishment, as he walked out the door he mentioned in a casual way, "I'll get back to you on that." And he was gone.

I found the nearest chair and plopped myself down in it with a great sigh of relief. What had just happened here? Who was this guy? How did he walk through a locked door? Where did that technology come from? More thoughts exploded in my mind until the one about reviewing the encounter made its way to the forefront. A "light-bulb-moment" flashed on in my head and I remembered the Super 8 camera on record mode. Vaulting out of my chair I raced to the shelf where the camera was still recording. Fumbling with the camera case, I finally got the film out and took it to be developed. It took four agonizing days before the small reel of developed film was back in my hands. I felt like a little boy at Christmas, anticipating what was in the packages about to be opened. My hands trembled as I threaded the film into the projector, but watching the replay was both exciting and disappointing. The holographic symbols and diagrams came out better than I thought but I failed to record the old man's face because he had his back or side toward the camera the whole time. When he wasn't near the desk he was not in the camera's viewfinder. I watched that short clip over and over for quite a while before my stomach finally insisted it needed nourishment.

A week went by, then two and three. Things were getting back to normal for me as a meat-cutter's apprentice. My job was to bone-out Utility and Cutter grades of beef for hamburger, mix that with white brisket fat and trim from the "Choice" and "Good" grades we sell to our customers. Then I had to blend them together by hand before emptying the tubs onto the meat-grinder tray for the first of two grindings. The good thing about being an apprentice is the hours spent alone in the cooler making hamburger. The bad thing is the cold aching fingers you get while mixing and remixing the meat.

When the hamburger is finished, the next task is placing frozen fish filets onto little blue trays. By the time that is completed, your fingers and hands are past aching and almost numb. The rest of the shift is completed with restocking the service counters, washing trays and tubs and cleaning the band saw and grinder. Not the most glamorous job but it does keep food on my table and a roof over my head. I have never been very socially active or aggressive which allowed more time for my hobby of being a UFO enthusiast. I looked into a group called MUFON but decided to find out as much as I could by myself. I knew if I joined a group, my lack of self-esteem would allow the group mentality, to influence my independence.

The next month completely changed my life. It all began when the same old man who took the pyramid from my desk entered the store where I worked. As I finished restocking and straightening the service counter I heard someone mention my complete name. The surprise of someone saying my middle name got my attention quickly. I didn't recognize him at first because his beard was neatly combed, he was wearing dark glasses and dressed in a business suit.

"Can we talk in your apartment in an hour?" he whispered.

A feeling somewhere between terror and panic raced through me but I acknowledged his request and nodded yes. He left the store quickly and my knees went weak. The next hour was the longest hour of my life. A knock at the door snapped me back to reality as I mustered as much poise as possible and responded, "Come in."

This time when he entered, he had a young man about my age with him, the younger man scanned the room with an instrument about the size of a deck of cards and declared the room was clean. (That was the first time anyone had accused my room of being clean.)

"What do you want with me?" I questioned.

"We have been watching you ever since you swept that field looking for the ***money clip***." The elderly gentleman continued, "We probably know more about you that you do."

Before he could say another word, I interrupted him, "Wait just a minute! What do you think you know about me?"

He got a little perturbed look on his face as he answered, "We know you were a sickly child, you had Scarlet Fever and almost died with double Pneumonia before you turned five years old. In grade school you bumped your mother while she was holding a pot of boiling water and spilled it on your head and shoulders; you thought you were going to be bald when they removed the bandages. In Jr. Hi, you discovered girls but were too self-conscious to even talk to them. In fact you didn't even go on a date or "sock-hop" all the way through high school. In the military . . . . "

I stopped him in mid sentence and questioned, "I don't know where you got that information but ***why*** would you want it?"

He answered, "If I succeed in recruiting you, I'll tell you; if not, there is no reason to tell you," then added, "I have been meeting with the Information Council and have persuaded them to answer your questions concerning what you saw in our holographic presentation." "I didn't understand anything I saw." then quickly added, "I'm not even sure I want to know."

"That is one reason we decided to tell you the whole story." he answered. "My purpose tonight is to ask you to accompany us for a ride you will surely tell to your grandchildren."

I liked the implication of living long enough to have grandchildren since I had never been married and didn't even have a girlfriend. I knew if they really wanted me to go with them, they could overpower me without much effort. The words, "ask you", eased my fears a little more but I needed a better reason to go willingly.

"What can't you tell me here that you can somewhere else?" I queered.

"We will not only to tell you but show you the things we say are true." he answered.

Since it was a Saturday, and I was off work Sunday, I requested a day to think about it. I felt a little disappointment in his voice when he told me if I didn't come with them now, he couldn't promise to come back Monday. They turned and he started to reach for the door knob when I impulsively responded, "OK! I'll come with you;" then I asked, "How long will this take?"

"As long as you want." was his response as we walked out the door.

Accompanying them down the stairs from the apartment, I questioned if I was making a fatally stupid move by allowing myself to do what I was doing. I was not an impulsive person, I don't just make snap decisions like this or go to unknown places with strangers; But here I was doing all that and not even packing a suitcase.

Reaching the building's front door and crossing the sidewalk, we were met by a powder blue Cadillac pulling up to the curb. As far back as I could remember I'd always thought owning a car like this would be the high point of my life. While I was sitting between the two men in the back seat of the car, the thought of how I let myself get into this ludicrous situation finally dawned on me. It seemed the more I was around these men the more questions I had. Not a word had been spoken until the car was half-way across the San Diego-Coronado Bay Bridge when I finally asked, "Okay, you've recruited me, why did you pick me?"

The bearded man turned to me and answered, "You only heard some of the things I found out, I also found no pattern of you lying or cheating; the only thing I did find was when you were about eleven, you stole a ten cent piece of fruit from a fruit stand after swimming one day but the next day you replaced it with a quarter. We need to find people who are fair-minded and will tell the truth after they see what you are about to see."

Satisfied for the moment, I asked where we were going. I didn't get an answer until we were crossing what looked like a golf course. "On a boat ride" was the answer.

An old feeling of discomfort started forming when the boat ride was mentioned. I served one term as a cook in the Army because in the Navy, boats have been known to sink and you end up in an ocean of water without a drop to drink or the Air Force because, what ever goes up, eventually comes down whether you want it to or not.

We turned left to cross a couple of channels before finally stopping at a gated slip near the north end of an island near Coronado Cays. I don't want to say I was scared, but I definitely wasn't thrilled to board the beautiful yacht they had waiting.

My fears were somewhat eased as seated before me were about twenty other people who were conversing, the few that looked up didn't seem as surprised to see me as I did them. They were talking to each other in different languages but all seemed to understand each other. No sooner did I notice this than the younger of my companions handed a small soft object that looked a lot like an eraser from a pencil. He just pointed to his ear and told me to insert it. Amazing! Through the left ear I heard gibberish but through the right ear I could understand what other people were saying. This new toy was so captivating that I didn't notice we were moving until I looked out a window as we cruised by an aircraft carrier across the bay. It wasn't long before we were passing Cabrillo National Monument and the Old Point Loma Light House. We were definitely heading for the rolling waves of the open ocean.

The yacht was heading directly toward the setting Sun. I had told some of the other passengers about the phenomena known as the Green Flash. Some of the passengers knew about it but almost half didn't so I asked them to followed me to the bow of the yacht where we awaited this phenomena. As we watched the Sun complete its daily journey of sinking into the Pacific Ocean and as the last rays disappeared over the horizon, chirps of excitement escaped from those who saw it for the first time. The California Coast was already swallowed up by the eastern horizon when the ship's speakers informed us to meet in the dining room for the evening meal.

I didn't know about the other "guests" but my meal was perfect: An inch thick grilled rib eye steak that had the marbling of a "Prime" beef, a perfect sized baked potato with all the condiments, and a glass of ice cold milk. The others must have enjoyed their meal also because this was the first time I have ever witnessed applause as the dinner plates were being removed and the dessert plates issued. I have never been big on dessert but this one seemed to evaporate in my mouth and leave a smooth sweet chocolate taste as I prepared for the next bite. As the dessert plates were being removed a numbered card was revealed under the plate. The card informed me of my cabin number. The card was reminiscent of the triangular face of the pyramid on my desk.

"Please return to the Lounge" boomed over the speakers so we all retired to the Lounge and sat around talking and sampling scrumptious drinks most of the night. I couldn't believe how interesting everyone was. In fact I was one of the last ones to find my room as the darkness of night was being invaded by strings of light heralding Sunday morning.

The most prevalent impression I gained that night was how similar we all were. I didn't agree with some of their ideas but the people could articulate valid reasons for their beliefs. I knew everyone there was smarter than me but they didn't make me feel inferior.

I missed breakfast the next morning but lunch made me think I was on a Cruise Ship. The food was fantastic. Around one o'clock we were escorted into a Conference Room, we sat there a few minutes while a few of the stragglers from last night made their appearance. All the chairs had occupants when a tall, fair-haired man with lightly tanned skin walked onto the stage. He stopped at the podium and asked for our attention. A hush crept over us as he began to speak,

"You are all wondering why you are here." Now there was total silence. He continued, "You are here to convince your fellow countrymen they are not alone on this planet and they are close to destroying it for everyone. If you don't stop polluting the air and water and start conserving the natural resources, this planet will not support life as you know it today. The good Ozone layer is our first line of defense against health damaging ultraviolet rays. Don't use wars to force your moral or ethical beliefs on other countries. We must learn to work together now or pay the price later. We want your cooperation on solving these and many more problems." He continued, "You may be the last group we make this attempt with. If you are not successful we may be forced to invade and that is the last thing we want to do." He ended his remarks with, "One final thought, may God be with you!"

A group of six men replaced the tall man on stage and instructed us to look at our room cards for further instructions. When I pulled mine out of my pocket it now read, "2nd of 3 on shuttle 5". "How do they do that?" I whispered.

Our whole group followed the leaders from the stage as they descended into the bowels of the ship. It became quite apparent what the room card meant as I stepped off the last rung of the stairs. Stretched out before me were five horizontal craft, each were shaped like cylinders that had been fitted with a base of a cone at each end. They were boarded by stepping through holes where windows should be located. I picked the cylinder with the big 5 on the roof and climbed through the "window" before sitting into the second of three passenger seats. Soon I was joined by two people I had met the night before. There were already two people in what could be called the pilot and co-pilot seats. The three of us tried to question the pilots to no avail. All of a sudden the windows closed and the bottom of the Yacht opened up like a clamshell and we slipped into the water. The silo-looking vessel was silent as we headed for a designation deep into the largest ocean on Earth. It wasn't long before the only light we could see was in our 'cabin'. I had no idea of speed because I couldn't see anything outside, but I could instinctively tell we were getting deeper. In what seemed to be only a few minutes a light on the nosecone illuminated the darkness. A small circular set of bright green strobe lights in the distance started blinking. The diameter of the circle of lights matched the diameter of our cylinder and we entered.

The lights from our craft revealed we were in a tunnel that looked to me like an empty lava tube and we were moving at a very rapid rate. As the tube twisted and turned we matched every turn with only inches to spare. All of a sudden we popped up to the surface again and found there was not only light but a whole city full of lights. Our craft was hoisted from the water and set on a cradle next to the dock. The windows retracted and we were told to exit.

Chapter 2

The Tour Begins

Waiting on the dock were three natives that looked a lot like us except they had bald heads, pale blue eyes and were wearing robes like the tall spokesman on the yacht. The closest person announced, "We are your guides for this time period." The guide that picked me was a few inches shorter than the others but had a nice smile and seemed to be friendly. His first remark was, "Welcome! I am your guide/host, I will answer your questions and explain your purpose for being here."

I wanted to ask right there how this small group of people could change anything, especially as important a task as was mentioned aboard the yacht, but decided to show patience instead. He motioned me to sit in a craft that was indubitably intended for two people. The double-walled shell was a clear plastic sphere, the top hemispheres opened on a nearly invisible hinge. When we entered, the hemisphere closed, the inner concentric sphere suspended itself a few inches from the outer sphere and the craft began to roll. I was told we were riding on an electro-magnetic wave between the passenger compartment and the exterior shell. There were no wheels since the outer sphere was the only thing touching the ground. It was exciting to ride in because the passengers were always sitting in the same position no matter if the vehicle was going up-hill, down-hill or around corners. It could be turned in any direction and the passengers automatically faced the direction it was heading.

"Where are we?" was my first question.

"This city doesn't have a dry-lander name. We don't use names here; there is no need for them." he replied.

"Then how do you tell someone who or where you are?" I questioned.

"I believe you call it telepathically. It is so much easier and I can talk to another person or a whole group of people if I feel the need."

"Can you talk to me telepathically?"

"I don't think so but I'll try . . . did you hear me?"

"No, I didn't even get static." The guide let out a chuckle and smiled at me.

"Where did you learn how to speak English?"

"I am in my last unit of education as a Communicator, I speak eight different Dry-Lander languages."

"So I'm a dry-lander?"

"Yes, I hope you don't mind that label"

"I've been called worse!"

"Worse? Is your name Worse?"

"No, that was just an attempt at humor, never mind."

As our bubble-car entered the arch to the city, I noticed an inscribed circle with a dolphin jumping through it. I was a little disappointed to see their city was not that different from our large cities, except this city was made entirely of a glass-like material with a light source that replaced the sky.

"Not much privacy here, is there?" I let slip out.

"Privacy? You want privacy?" with a flip of a switch the clear glass turned black and the car stopped immediately.

"How in the world did you do that?" I exclaimed.

With an inflection of superiority he retorted, "A small electrical charge makes the difference." It seemed my guide had a short fuse when it came to criticizing his city. Something for me to remember if I was going to keep an open dialog with him!

"Want something to eat?" he suggested. I hadn't eaten since lunch on the yacht and felt the need to accept his request. "This is a good place" he said as we rolled into a parking spot shaped like a soup bowl sunk into the ground up to its rim. Getting out of the vehicle was easy because the seats swiveled and tilted almost ejecting the passenger.

The food in the restaurant was the blandest meal I'd ever eaten but he seemed to like it.

"How did you like it?" he asked.

"Very filling" I responded, remembering my earlier criticism. I noticed we didn't get a bill at the end of the meal and I didn't see him pay either. When asked about it, he matter-of-factually said no one pays to eat. My "Wet-Lander" economics lesson went something like this:

"What do you pay for?"

"Nothing"

"How does that work?"

"Do you want the short version?"

"Yes."

"Every one of us has a job of one kind or another and through the combination of all our skills we provide everything needed to sustain our society."

"I don't get it."

"Ok, I'll start at the beginning. When a child is born, the mother and father are relieved of their work duties until the child is taught how to focus his/her telepathic abilities. When the child can communicate at a prescribed level, the child enters the pre-educational phase of their lives while the father and mother return to our workforce. It is this phase's responsibility to teach social and mental skills until the child demonstrates a readiness to enter the education phase of life. I am now in that final stage and here we are."

"So you were born; that implies your mother and father had sex."

"That's obvious. What is your question?"

"You caught me off guard. I just didn't think of you as sexual beings." As soon as those words left my mouth I knew I'd stepped on his toes again.

"I've seen documentaries on dry-landers excess in sexual pursuits, your preoccupation with sexual fantasies and the time you waste trying to find sexual pleasure with each other. Why do you waste so much time on a purely biological function?"

I wanted to say because we have an abundance of beautiful women where I come from and if he was any indication of the average Joe here, I was in no hurry to meet the female population. It was a good thing he couldn't read my mind. Regaining my composure, my response was: "You're right. We probably do spend too much time fantasizing."

It was probably that bland meal that directed my attention away from noticing the females in that restaurant because I couldn't recall any females in there that had bumps on their robes in the right places. I was too occupied gagging down the meal. I continued: "Let's drop that subject and return to a more important topic." He agreed.

"If nobody pays for anything, how does your economy work?"

"Very simply! As we develop during our education period, we show tendencies toward certain occupations. With guidance we finally select the field in which we are most interested and begin work. If we find we have made a mistake, we return to the education mode and try again. We have jobs for everyone and everyone has a job and since nothing we want costs 'money', we don't need a currency."

"That sounds a lot like a barter system to me."

"Not exactly, but there are similarities."

"So you are telling me that some of your people would rather pick up garbage than be a Communicator like you?"

"Not exactly, of course the more popular jobs are filled first with the most qualified people so we have more 'perks', as you call them, for the less popular occupations.

"What kind of perks do you offer?"

"The most popular ones are trips during non-work periods, with Space Flight being the most desirable."

"You mean you can actually fly into Space?" The guide chuckled a little louder this time.

"How do you think we got here in the first place?" Boy! Did I feel stupid, but continued: "Then you are the guys flying around in those UFO's we've been seeing for years."

"Not exactly, there are five cultures from our planet under the oceans and seas of this planet."

"And you all get along without any problems?"

"Not exactly!" He was starting to get on my nerves with his, "Not exactly" bit.

"What does, not exactly, mean?"

"Well, on our home planet the ones you call the Grays, were the most primitive culture we had. In fact they lived deep under our planet's surface in tunnels and caves. They had almost no technology and were by far the smallest group in our convoy. This made their trip here a lot more difficult and frustrating. Maybe that is why they are a little more reckless. They insist on flying during the daylight hours and have even abducted dry-landers for personal research. We have offered them all the knowledge we have on humans but they claim our knowledge isn't relative to their situation. I don't know if they just don't trust us or are too proud to accept our help. Our Information Council has made it quite clear that no dry-landers are to be injured or killed and they have agreed. I do know they want a colony on the surface but have still not adjusted to the 78% Nitrogen level in the atmosphere like the rest of us. It seems the closer to solving their problem they get, the more chances they take.

"It's just a good thing we have had people in right places to minimize the reporting and social impacts of their recklessness. You helped us out by publishing Project Blue Book which made people who reported seeing UFO's seem like they were mentally disturbed. We feel it is inevitable that someone is going to get hurt if we don't step in and prepare you for their coming to the surface."

"That's a lot for me to digest, I mean, think about."

We sat quietly in the 'car' for a while. Finally my guide admitted he had probably told me too much too soon and he would take me to my room for the sleep period.

As we were walking up the stairs to my room, I suddenly remembered I had to be to work in the morning. I exclaimed my concern; he turned and told me they had already taken care of it. "What did you tell them?" I inquired.

"Your work was told you had just won a cruise around the world and wouldn't be back for a month."

"Are they going to keep my job open for me?"

"I doubt it, they didn't seem to be concerned about that."

Great! Now I was on the bottom of the Pacific Ocean without a job, no clean clothes and a story nobody would believe. The more I thought of my predicament, the funnier it sounded. By the time we reached my door I just had to laugh out loud. My guide must have jumped a foot in the air.

"What are you doing?" he exclaimed.

"Laughing at the irony of this situation, who would ever believe the truth?" I responded. As we walked down the hall, I asked him why he jumped when he heard me laugh? He replied it was only because he was concentrating on something else and was caught off guard.

Walking through the open door to my room, the guide informed me this was a Guest Room for visiting Dry-Landers. He informed me it was quite similar to his room except I needed a remote to do my bidding because of my limitations. I knew what he meant but let it slide. I wasn't sure I could get along with this guy for a whole month if he continued talking down to me, but I kept my mouth shut.

The room was remarkably similar to mine in San Diego. Except this one had a built-in TV next to the table. It was like my room in that it also had two chairs, a sink, cupboards, a bed with a nightstand and a dresser. The only odd piece of furniture was the rectangular box in the corner near the window, it looked like a photo booth you would find at an amusement park. The floor and walls were painted but the outside wall was completely clear. I looked at the outside wall and then at him but I didn't want to get into that privacy thing again so I didn't say a word. I didn't have to because he told me to push the 'window' button on the remote and see what happens. I did and the clear glass turned dark, the ceiling lit up brighter and a superior smile crept across his face again.

"Before I leave, you may want me to show you how your remote works?" he said with his grin getting bigger.

"I'm pretty tired," I mentioned as I yawned politely. Besides, all the buttons on the remote were written in English.

"Then I'll see you in the waking phase, good-bye." He exited the room.

Finally I was alone again. I looked at the remote and decided to try a few buttons so I pushed 'lights' and they dimmed a little. Again I depressed the button and again they dimmed. If the button was held down, the lights would continue to dim until they went off, but if the button was not released at that point, they would return to full brightness. Next I pushed 'shower' and a sliding door on half the 'photo booth' slid open to reveal a shower. After closing the shower door, I was about to push 'toilet' button but decided it was obvious what it would reveal. There were a few more buttons on the remote but they looked self-explanatory too so I set it on the nightstand.

I tried lying on the bed but my mind wouldn't let go of the experiences I'd witnessed this day. While I pulled the blanket up to my chest and tried to relax by cradling my head in my hands, I noticed my wristwatch for the first time since this whole journey began. Now I could tell the date and time it was back home and wondered if this place was in a different time zone. Only a tired person would have such a weird thought. I had been gone only two days but the sight of something familiar calmed my nerves enough to let me sleep.

According to my watch, six and a half hours had passed before waking and feeling well rested. I seemed to be making a habit of missing at least one meal a day but it was definitely time to endure another meal here. I found toothpaste and a brush next to the sink but I needed a shower first. Pushing the 'shower' button, the door slid open again, revealing a shower similar to one you would find at a motel, complete with soap, shampoo and hand lotion. That's where the similarity ended. I stepped inside with my shorts on. The door automatically slid close and the shower covered me with tepid water. I tried to open the door but couldn't so I got out of my shorts with as much dignity as I could muster, finally enjoying the rest of my shower when the water reached a more comfortable temperature. I instinctively tried to turn the water off but it went off by itself, which triggered a blast of warm air to shoot out of the walls, floor and ceiling, covering my whole body for about twenty seconds. Then the door opened and I stepped out. I felt like I had just been through a car wash and blown dry.

After the shower I wrung out my shorts, tossed them into a corner and walked across the room where I found a robe with a pair of shorts on the bed where my clothes had been. Someone had entered my room while I was taking the shower and replaced my clothes with a traditional robe. "When in

Rome . . ." flashed in my mind. Finishing my oral hygiene, I strolled toward the door expecting it to open automatically, it didn't. In fact there was no handle on this side like on the other when we entered. I won't say I panicked but my adrenalin level was elevated as I searched the area around the door with my hands. Not finding a lever or button to open the door I wandered back to the bed and sat down. Pondering my next move, my eyes spotted the remote on the table. Maybe it has a "help" button. It didn't but it did have a "door" button. Pushing it a few times resulted in the door's opening and closing a few times. I noticed some other interesting buttons, like the one for 'food'. I pushed it and immediately the portion of the wall behind the table lit up a big-screen TV and a robust man in an apron appeared. In a pleasing voice he asked if I had a restful night's sleep and was I now ready to eat something. He looked so real I almost went over to touch him but realized that would be sophomoric. I didn't remember what my guide ordered yesterday but I didn't want that anyway, so I asked,

"What are my options?"

He answered, "Anything you want."

"How about two chicken eggs (who knows what animal they get eggs from down here), two strips of bacon, hash brown potatoes, one piece of white bread with strawberry jam and a cup of coffee?"

"Thank you, I'll be at your door shortly." (I almost said my name wasn't 'shortly' but knew he wouldn't get the joke) About five minutes later there was a knock at my door and the same gentleman I had talked to entered my room, set down a tray on the table that had everything I ordered and left. It was hot and delicious. Now I knew why my guide had that smirk on his face since 'lunch'.

No sooner had I finished than a knock on the door revealed the 'waiter' returning for the empty tray and dishes. He smiled and asked if I enjoyed the meal. I answered in the affirmative and thanked him. As he was leaving the room he turned toward me and said, "May God be with you." and he was gone.

That was the second reference to God I'd heard from these people. I had assumed since their technical advancement was far greater than ours they would have out-grown God or at least thought of themselves as Godlike.

Chapter 3

Their History

My first question when the guide entered the room was, "Will you tell me about your religion?"

"Okay . . . . We can start our tour later, what do you want to know?"

"Anything you care to tell me."

"Okay, I'll start back on our home planet."

"That sounds like a good place to start."

"Before our deliverance, our political situation was about where Earth's governments are now. Our differences between cultures, economic advantages and religions kept wars springing up one after the other. Some cultures just wanted to be left alone, we wanted to help everyone to be free just like we were and of course there were those who wanted to rule our whole planet.

As our technology advanced, we developed bombs that could create 'land-quakes" and GEMS (Gravitational-Electro-Magnetic System) beams that could direct near-by asteroids to rain-down on our enemies with pin-point accuracy. We used that technology to proclaimed to our enemy that God was on our side and was punishing them for their actions against us.

That worked for a while but it wasn't long before some of our "Peace Activists" acted on the idea that if our enemies had the same knowledge, that would level out the playing field and each side would be afraid to attack the other which would result in worldwide peace. With their help, it didn't take long for our enemies to develop similar technology and begin hitting us with larger meteorites. Finally our planet couldn't take it any more and started developing mega quakes with huge fissures opening up and volcanoes erupting more violently on every continent."

"When all seemed hopeless, God appeared everywhere on our planet at the same time and stopped the carnage with an uplifted hand. Everyone stopped what they were doing and looked skyward, fixing their eyes on Him. At that moment He gave everyone the ability to telepathically communicate with Him. Everyone on the planet saw their whole life flash through their minds and God judged them. Some ascended, most stayed on the ground. The ones who ascended said they could hear the ones left behind yelling and screaming and asking for forgiveness but it was too late.

All the people who ascended were assembled into huge space ships that appeared out of nowhere. God announced to them they were chosen to go to a planet He called Earth.

The journey would take many generations and be filled with many learning situations but He would send Angels to guide and help them. He didn't say why He didn't just teleport them to Earth but they found out later. Before God sent them on their way He let them watch the rest of Judgment Day."

"From their vantage point, they saw people popping out of the ground like popcorn on a hot skillet and others were shooting up through the surface of our waters like huge raindrops being filmed in reverse. Soon the sky was filled with His true believers as they ascended to Him. God spoke to the people who had ascended and said, "You are my chosen ones and will dwell with Me in Heaven." Before God and His believers left, He lifted his other arm and the whole planet became engulfed in fire, even the atmosphere caught on fire. Our whole planet was destroyed in a blink of an eye and was reduced to nothing more than a huge fireball."

"While still in orbit, God gave the directive, 'I have already let life evolve on Earth to a point at which you will join the evolution, you will not destroy or enslave any person on Earth. You will be my caretakers until man is ready.'

Only then did He send the ships on their journey. Almost everyone in our convoy felt pangs of sorrow as they watched their burning planet shrink to a dot of light and then disappear altogether."

"I can't imagine how difficult it would be to watch your planet burst into flame like that."

"As caretakers, we were directed to not let that happen here."

"Sounds like history is about to repeat itself doesn't it?"

"Not if we can help it! That is the main purpose you are here. We are trying to show you a better way before it comes to that."

"One more question!"

"Okay!"

"Why do you think God picked your ancestors from different religions for the journey? Many of our religions believe they are the only "true" religion and everyone else will end up in Hell."

"Our ancestors asked themselves the same question and it took years to answer. In fact it was that idea that led to the formation of our Information

Council, but to answer your question. It was concluded that the only things all these people had in common was, each of them believed in only one God even if they had different names for Him and they made an honest attempt to live in such a way as to include Him and His teachings in their daily lives."

There was a long pause in the conversation while I thought about what he just said. Then we continued our conversation with me asking, "How is your government structured?"

"You mean our Council . . . I'll give you the quick course of our politics. On the trip here, our ancestors asked each other why they felt they were the ones chosen and decided to poll everybody. Even though each of us had retained the ability to communicate telepathically, it didn't work very well because there were just too many people to hear each one individually. Then they decided to have each deck of each ship pick a 'Spokesman' which led to the spokesmen picking an 'Overseer' for the whole ship. The Overseers met to form our first 'Council' which evolved into our present 'Culture Council'. Then the Culture Council selects members to sit on other councils like the Information Council, the Educational Council, etc."

"So you're telling me your 'Culture Council' thinks we are wrecking Earth and may invade us dry-landers if we can't solve our current problems?"

"Not exactly, first of all, Earth is not **just** your planet; we live here too. We have been working on these problems for quite a while and have a few solutions to try before anything that drastic happens."

"Like what?"

"We have infiltrated every segment of your society by developing cosmetic skills that make it almost impossible for you to tell the difference between you and us. We have used these people to infiltrate many walks of your life, even positions of power in some of your governments and military. We have been part of your life from the beginning of your recorded history."

"Just how long have you lived among us?" I asked.

With a growing smile on his face my guide replied: "Quite a while, I believe you call us the missing link. We are amazed that you keep trying to manipulate history in order to 'prove' you are ancestors of monkeys and some-how they developed into Neandertal Man, and finally Homo-sapiens that jumped out of the trees of pre-history and into documented city-states like the Greeks and Romans developed.

We thought you would have figured out by now that God has been around since what you call "The Big Bang." It is written in the first book of your Bible, "And God said, Let there be light: and there was light." "At first I took that statement to simply mean God separated daylight from nighttime but the more I thought about it, the more it sounds like a description of the Big Bang Theory." Before I could form a thought, he continued,

"We all seem to have a hard time understanding the Bible because when God inspired the writing of the books that became the Canon of your Bible, you forgot it was written in terms the people of that day could understand. By the time the scholars decided which books should be included, some words used at the time had changed meaning before the Bible was finalized . . . but His Love and desire for you to follow his Commandments were then and are now crystal clear."

"I'm confused, are you saying the Bible is not completely true?"

"No! What I am saying is, just because we don't understand or can't comprehend every word or story in the Bible doesn't mean it's not true."

"I have had people tell me the story of Adam & Eve is just a story, they say that bones of prehistoric man prove Adam or Eve was not the first man or woman on Earth."

"We have heard the same argument. The thing they don't know is that the bones they found and are finding now were not from the first humanoids to walk this Earth. We have found humanoid settlements that date back to your Mesozoic Period and they probably left because of the dinosaurs.

Another thing they don't understand is that Adam and Eve were the fist humans that God created and made a covenant with on this planet. So they were the first true man and woman on Earth to experience His presence. God is a lot greater and has created a lot more than just your species. The more I deal with you humans, the harder it is for me to understand why God keeps his covenants with you."

I figured this would be a good time to change the subject back to what we were talking about before the Bible lesson.

"So, you are saying your cultures have been on Earth before Adam and Eve, and that you are the "Missing Link?" That means you have been here for what? At least fifty thousand years?"

"Now you are putting words in my mouth, we have been here many thousands of your years and you are the one that called us the missing link. We are not consumed with the idea of dating non-personal sections of time like your culture does. But if you are curious about how humans developed on Earth, I'll tell you."

"I'm all ears, I mean yes."

"You developed by being related to every living creature on this earth, under the seas and in the air. You come from God as does everything else in this universe."

"It is good that you question things, I am surprised you haven't learned by now that for every question your mind finds a suitable answer; *that answer* exposes many more questions and this process hasn't led to the conclusion you are not alone in the Universe."

"So are you saying we should stop asking questions and learning?"

"Not exactly, I'm saying learning is infinite and the more you learn the more you should realize how little you know."

"Oh! The smarter we get the stupider we are?"

"Stop trying to put words in my mouth, I definitely wouldn't put it like that but apparently you would. (It looked like I was finally finding a humanoid temper in this guy) Quickly he regained his composure and continued, "As I was saying, since our well-being is linked to yours, we need to work together in order to survive; but I'll get into that later."

I was glad he was changing the subject because this conversation was going down hill fast. He surprised me by being able to pick up our conversation where we left off before the historical / religious conversation. (He had to be very disciplined in order to pick up his story like he did)

He continued, "Our convoy of refugees spent fourteen generations in Space. Now that we had the new-found ability to communicate telepathically with each other, we learned to respect each other's point of view on about everything physical, mental and spiritual. We finally came to the realization that all the different cultures were like one body with each culture being one part of that body. Much like an arm, leg, hand or foot being part of a human's body. If you are missing one part, that diminishes the whole body and even if the smallest part is not functioning properly, the whole body is affected. God told us He had already set humans on an evolutionary track and we were to join with them in their evolution; but as each generation passed, we were beginning to wonder if we would ever reach the Promised Land called Earth. When we finally saw Earth, almost every one of us fell to our knees and thanked God for bringing us to such a beautiful place."

"I noticed you referred to the people on the journey as **us**, you did mean your ancestors didn't you?"

"Of course . . . . Do I really look **that** old?"

"Excuse me, that was a stupid question. Please continue."

"After all our ships obtained orbit, we picked out areas on Earth that most resembled places described to us by our elders back on our home planet and landed to begin our new lives."

"Is that why you live under the Pacific Ocean now?"

"No." (Boy was I glad he didn't say "not exactly" again.)

"What happened then?" I continued.

"Some ships landed as far away from humans as possible, which was hard to do because the humans were spread out over the best land to find food. Others landed closer and began mixing with humans right from the start. We have always had a longer life span than humans and that turned out to be a detriment instead of an advantage. Humans with the shorter lifespan, reproduced a lot quicker and more often so it became a numbers game. We were helping humans make us obsolete as a people simply by helping them control their environment. We decided that since over 70% of Earth is covered by water, and humans didn't have the ability to follow us, we would develop our civilization under the oceans or on islands instead of the mainland."

"I can't believe we pushed you into the sea."

"Pushed? I don't think so, we remembered the directive from God when He told us not to harm or enslave you. We have lived up to that directive to the best of our abilities."

"Is that the whole story of how you ended up here on the bottom of the largest ocean in the world?"

"Not exactly, my culture landed on an island in what is now called the Mediterranean Sea. We kept to ourselves and since we were out of reach of the humans, we developed a very affluent society. We were much more advanced than the rest of you so we began to think too highly of ourselves. We knew we lived on a volcano but believed we could control it. For generations we had used its energy to let us produce products that could not be found anywhere else on Earth. "Eventually, some of our people on the outer ring, traded with some outsiders for exotic fruits and spices for our tables and animals for our zoos but we never let the outsiders past the outer ring of our city. Since our central city was secure from all outside influences, this gave our scientists time to develop many wondrous inventions. Some of our citizens were so proud of our accomplishments they would bring outsiders to our second ring so they could be impressed by our achievements like flying machines, submarines and what they called our horseless carts."

"How did the outsiders react when they saw the differences between their lives and yours?"

"They were astonished and couldn't believe their eyes: When our Elders heard about it they were furious. They asked the merchants what they were thinking by letting outsiders into the second ring and putting us in danger like that?" The reply was, "We don't understand why that would be putting us all in danger. First of all, what other outsider would believe their stories of our technology and wealth; besides if any of them did try to invade, our superior technical knowledge would have no problem defeating them.' That answer really enraged the elders who replied, 'Don't you remember our basic directive? We can't use our superior strength to harm the outsiders."

"It surprises me that someone with that clear of an advantage would honor the directive."

"You have to remember our ancestors saw first-hand what happened when our home-planet was destroyed and we what were told concerning this planet."

"Anyway, the way things turned out, any invasion proved to be a moot point. A few years after that, one of the new defensive experiments being developed for our protection malfunctioned, which triggered the volcano to erupt, destroying everything we had built. It was just by the grace of God that many of my ancestors were sightseeing around the world when our volcano island exploded. The obliteration was so complete that it killed every inhabitant before causing a great tsunami and sinking into the sea."

"That sounds a lot like Homer's Atlantis to me."

"Could be, only three other cultures had similar cities around the world and Homer might have been describing one of them."

"Then you are the survivors of Atlantis?"

"We might be."

Chapter 4

Tour of the City

A long silence found its way into the conversation. Finally he asked, "Do you want a tour of the city?" I confirmed that would be nice so as I looked for the 'door' button on the remote, he opened the door without touching it and we left the room.

The first business we visited was a garment factory. People were sewing different fabrics together, constructing the traditional robes, business suits, dresses and many outfits that were foreign to me. Looking at the variety of garments on the tables, I inquired as to why there were so many different types of clothing when everyone I'd met wore the same white robes? His reply was that this factory makes garments for not only our culture but for all diplomatic missions to the dry-landers around the world. Then he added, "They will make one for me as soon as I decide where I want to do my service."

I didn't want to get him started on what "his service" really meant so I asked how each worker knew when his or her 'shift' was over. The guide replied they were given a list of garments to finish and when that list was complete, they were finished for the phase and wouldn't have to return until their next cycle.

"How do they know when their next cycle for work starts?" I inquired.

"When a person finished the required output for their phase, they contact the person designated to replace them 'telepathically' and decide the particulars on making the transition." That sounded very unorganized to me but it seemed to be working for them.

"What do they do when they are not working?" I asked.

"The same things you dry-landers do." was the answer.

"Wait a minute, we can go hunting, fishing, skiing, sky-diving or a lot of other things. You just don't have the room to do them here."

"We can do all that and much more."

"How?"

Our next stop was at a building with a large trisected circle engraved above the doorway. He referred to as their Sports Complex. My curiosity got the better of me and I asked if the three sectors had any significance?

"They stand for Land, Water and Air" was his reply. And then added, "You'll see why in a little while."

As we entered the building it did not look like there was enough room to play any sport I knew. All I could see were three hallways with doors every twenty feet or so on each side of the halls. My guide directed me to a chest-high desk to the left of the door, manned by the most attractive female I had seen here.

"In what recreational activity do you feel like participating?" my guide requested.

I figured I would stump him right off the bat so I said, "Hang-gliding." The receptionist began typing on the console in front of her and a card popped up. The guide gave her a quick glance and we proceeded down the hall to a door that didn't have a blinking light next to the card receptacle. As he inserted the card, a menu lit up with all kinds of symbols I couldn't read. The guide pushed a few buttons and the door opened.

"I hope you don't mind if I accompany you, I haven't used this program in quite a while." he requested. The door closed and we found ourselves about ten feet from the edge of a cliff overlooking a valley with huge monoliths and a river winding through them. It was breathtaking. Resting on stands were two hang gliders that looked a lot like Willis Wing birds with all the hardware. All this looked too authentic to me. I knew we entered a room so this couldn't be real.

"Holographic projection?" I squeaked.

"Pretty neat! Isn't it?" he replied.

We got hooked up in our harnesses and I told him to go first. I couldn't believe it. After he stepped off the cliff he disappeared for a few seconds until his glider caught enough air to bring him back into view. As I watched, he kept getting smaller as he sailed away. I couldn't chicken-out now so I got a little run before launching. This was unbelievable, I felt the same rush of adrenaline, wind in my face, riding the updrafts and freedom I felt soaring near La Jolla, California. We sailed quite a while before my guide noticed one of the monolithic rocks had a donut-hole in it and he guided his bird right through the middle. I was too high so I circled once before following through the center. A short time later we sat the gliders down near the river on a nice sandy beach. I was pumped! We congratulated each other after landing and I thanked him profusely. One thing strange was that we ended up at the back wall of the room, and if this whole thing was just an illusion, how did we move? I didn't ask, I was just exhilarated. Of course the lights came on; we left the room and returned the card to the young woman behind the desk. She looked at us and said, "Come on back anytime." I knew she must have been talking to me because there was no need to speak to my guide.

Walking out the door my guide quipped, "I think she likes you." I must have blushed a little because the smile on his face broadened into a little chuckle.

The next few sleep phases were spent going to old movie theatres, stage performances,(they actually talked out loud while performing) and even going to a museum. I asked why they had movie theatres when they had those great holographic programs back at the Sports Complex? His response was that the older citizens preferred movies because they illustrated the struggles and history of our home planet before we destroyed it.

"How did you acquire the information for these movies?" I asked.

"Our people had a long time to write everything they could remember about our planet, it was reviewed by each of the other groups, adjusted and corrected before it was sent to each ship for the acceptance vote. If the majority of each ship endorsed it, only then was it included into the official canon of our history."

"That sounds interesting, can we just walk in and sit down?"

"Okay,(then a short pause) if you want to see, The Battle of Guildemesh."

"Sounds bloody and gory to me."

"It is and I hope you have the stomach for it."

As we entered the theatre, I expected to see a snack bar with pop, candy and popcorn but instead we walked through an empty foyer and right into a large room with a huge battle raging where the back wall should be and 150 to 200 fold-down seats arranged into about a 90 degree arc. The "movie" was playing but there was no sound. I looked at my guide and he told me I had to just watch because the sound track was telepathically transmitted. (I wanted to ask how that was possible but decided to watch the production instead). As we were sitting down I heard some people moan as a huge fireball exploded in the middle of a village, sending bodies hurling through the air. Other scenes depicted prisoners being tortured in horrible ways to the point I asked my guide if we could leave.

"I warned you it would be bad." he consoled.

"Why in the world would you let such a terrible sight be shown?"

"We let our people see how demeaning war is in order to remind them how painful it is to let situations escalate to the point of combat. Everything you saw did happen and will happen again if we can't learn from our past mistakes."

"I was in the Army for a while but never encountered anything close to what I just saw."

"Consider yourself lucky then, because many of those people's distant relatives lived through those horrific times."

"Are all your movies like that?"

"First of all, what you just saw was not a movie, it was a Computerized Holographic Production with a Synchronized Telepathic Recording; Second, of course not, we have every type of movie you have except the sexually explicit ones."

"In that case, who is your favorite actor or actress?"

"You mean real people like our Stage Actors and Actress'?"

"No, who is your favorite male or female Movie Actor?"

"I've already told you we don't have live actors or actresses, all our movies are computer generated down to the last detail."

"Computer generated? What's that?"

"A computer is a machine that can be programmed to illustrate anything we want it to display."

"Programmed?"

"I think we had better drop the explanation, I don't think I can explain the process well enough for you to understand."

"You are probably right. So you don't have a favorite!"

"That's right, because the images don't act, they only seem to be real because someone has telepathically recorded a message that follows the action on the screen."

"Boy! They sure seemed real to me."

"That's the whole point, isn't it?" he sarcastically noted.

It was time to move on because their movies were too graphic and I didn't care for the stage performances; so he took me to a museum.

The first museum was "Earth History of Mankind." It seems their recollection of history doesn't coincide with ours very well. The way they explained it was there is no "missing link." There are monkeys, apes and man, not one evolving into the other.

The guide went on to explain: "Some of the people you call pre-historic were actually very intelligent space travelers when they left from their home planet. We theorize their main problem was they were among the first space travelers to leave their respective space programs and were not properly prepared for the generational length of the journey. They didn't take into effect the prolonged lack of gravity on their body."

"We found the magnetic boots they wore were intended to provide a gravity substitute but were probably uncomfortable and awkward so they spent most of the time floating from station to station as they maintained the ship. Most had hibernation capsules installed for prolonged flight but the trip took so long that the capsules woke them as they began to malfunction. By the time the species arrived in orbit around this planet the offspring looked nothing like the scientists that started the journey, they looked more like beasts than people. They lacked the skill and strength to land the craft, only a few were able to crash-land their craft and survive. The survivors were weak and had trouble adjusting to Earth's environment. Also their craft was damaged to the point they could only use it for shelter. Eventually they had to venture outside and take their chances with the local flora and fauna."

"On our planet, we had a fringe group of scientists who had a dooms-day mentality and banded together under a charismatic leader who preached peace, love and the need to get off our planet before it was too late. They didn't believe in weapons so their expedition didn't bring weapons of any kind."

"As I said, it took fourteen generations for us to get here and it must have taken them a few more so you can imagine how surprised we were when we actually discovered their wreckage.

I noticed the display of the members of this early expedition didn't look like my guide at all, they looked more like a Neanderthal or Cro-Magnon Man. When I asked the guide about the similarity he got a little defensive. He told me the tests on these bones proved a common ancestry to them but something happened during the trek that altered their appearance in a significant way. He blamed the small number of travelers caused the inbreeding of their offspring and the lack of gravity during their long trip. Then he added, "We don't recognize your Neanderthal or any of the other species including your Homo Sapiens as true mankind. I was a little mystified that he would offer such a brief explanation but decided to let it go since I could tell it bothered him; besides, I felt he knew our Neanderthal, Cro-Magnon Man and Homo-sapiens were really *his* scientist's expedition.

The next display followed the migration of their population as it grew and spread outward from what is now central Africa, North and East, to what is now Europe and Asia. They claim as they moved, they adapted to the environment and that change in environment and breeding with the locals seemed to have an accelerated effect on genetic mutations. Only the smarter and stronger mutations survived with the weaker ones dying out. The last display featured agriculture changing the hunter into a farmer and that leading to the formation of towns and cities.

The first display in the next museum was a huge variety of weapon-looking devices. I believe my first words were, "Wow! Great weapons!" My guide was quick to point out that those were not weapons but tools used to create a better life. There was an exo-skeletal device that increased the wearer's strength twenty fold for lifting or moving heavy objects. There were rifle sized, ray-gun looking devices that could melt solid rock, hand held devices which when aimed at an object would make certain objects lose a measure of its gravitational attraction and float in thin air.

"Our architects used these machines to lift thirty-ton blocks while helping build the original Giza Pyramids, making sure the airshafts pointed to the three stars in Orion's Belt so no one would ever forget the direction from which they came." He quickly added that they didn't help build all the pyramids in Egypt or in the rest of the world.

When I asked him about the pyramids in South America and the geoglyphs found near Nasca, he got an annoyed look on his face and told me that was one of the reasons all the cultures decided to move to the oceans.

"I don't understand? How could pictographs make you move?"

"You already know of the Nasca Lines so I'll tell you the story. One of our ships landed in a desert in Peru and had a good life for themselves until some of the locals found them and saw how rich our life had become. It was impossible to keep the natives away so we made the mistake of educating them, which changed their whole life. The more they learned the more they used their knowledge to create a society that was far advanced from other natives. Our greatest fears were realized when they began to dominate other tribes in the region. We didn't see any other scenario but to end the damage we created by moving somewhere they couldn't follow. Later flights over the area revealed they drew pictures using small rocks that could only be seen from the sky. We figured the pictures were for our benefit but we never landed there again."

The next museum we were to visit was their R & D museum. We were just starting the tour through the Technological Museum of Research & Development when all of a sudden my guide stopped in mid-sentence, got this solemn look on his face and in a calm and disciplined voice, announced, "I have to leave, my grandfather just died." I started to ask how he knew but realized the answer so I didn't. "Go!" I said, "I can take care of myself." He left and I kept visualizing the semi-controlled emotional look on my guide's face as he received the news of his grandfather. For some unexplained reason I felt empathy for his situation and had no desire to complete the tour.

Since the guide took the "bubble-mobile", I decided to walk back to the "guest room".

Heading in the direction I hoped was my room, I kept noticing passer-bys looking at me and then turning away quickly. I probably needed a haircut and I knew I needed a shave; finally a young boy came up to me and asked if he could touch my hair. Not knowing what else to do, I bent over and he put his hand on my face and began petting me like a dog. His mother rushed over and grabbed him while apologizing profusely. After calming her down by telling her I wasn't offended, I asked for directions to the dry-lander's guest room. She gave me detailed directions and then continued to reprimand her son as I walked off. That incident spurred my curiosity about the youngster's odd action. As I walked, I noticed about 4 out of 5 people had the hood on their robes covering their head. The other 20% looked like they had a fine head of hair. Not until I reached for the door latch to my room did I think of reaching for my door keys. Of course I was wearing a robe with pockets but had no keys. That was when I first thought about security. There was a handle but no place for a key on the outside so I decided to check the other doors down the hall. There was no slot for keys on them either. I didn't have anything worth stealing anyway, since I hadn't packed a suitcase or even taken my camera, so I turned the handle and entered.

Maybe it was entering the room by myself, but this time it looked a lot more sterile. I couldn't believe I was getting a little home sick for my messy, dirty and poorly lit room back in Diego. The remote was on the table right where I had left it so I picked it up and pushed 'food'. The same pleasant looking man asked what I would like to eat. Thinking a minute, I ordered spaghetti with meatballs and a large beer. We thanked each other and I waited for a knock on my door. While waiting I wondered what was on 'TV' so I pushed the appropriate button. This time the screen on the wall doubled in size and the program in progress was something about roller coasters. Only when these roller coasters came at me I actually flinched while trying to jump out of the way. It had to be 3-D-TV with sound all around me. The picture was as clear as if I was standing on the tracks. Not only that, I could smell popcorn and cotton candy.

I had barely recovered from that experience when the man with the food knocked on the door. I invited him in and he set the food on the table and turned to leave. Impulsively, I asked him if he could stay for a while and talk. He politely refused saying he had his duties to complete before he had any free time. After he left, I couldn't believe I'd asked someone to keep me company. That was 'so' unlike me; I enjoyed being alone back in San Diego. The spaghetti tasted okay but wasn't as good as my mother's but at least the beer tasted good. I could tell the remote control was going to be my best friend tonight but only after I had a shower. It was in the shower, while washing my ears, I felt that eraser-thing I'd inserted while on the yacht. Not taking any chances on losing it down the drain, I removed it and set it in the soap dish. After the shower and being blown dried, I reinserted the communicator, slipped into some shorts and sat on the bed. I began surfing through sports, news, movies and educational channels until I got to a travel channel.

The feature was about different trips that could be taken on free time periods. They had short, intermediate and long period trips offered. The short trip started with beautiful underwater views of rock formations that looked like stalagmites rising from the bottom of the ocean with whales flying between and around them like giant birds looking for a place to land. I was amazed how graceful these huge creatures were. How they could take pictures in that deep of water was astounding to me. There were other short trips but that one I found the most interesting.

The Intermediate trip I liked most was a night trip to the dry-lander's largest cities with layovers during the daylight hours in remote forests with guided tours of exotic animals of the region. Most of the animals on that program I had never seen before.

I don't know how long the 'long' trip takes (in fact they didn't say how long any of the trips took.) but I can see why these people would save their free time until they could accumulate enough for this trip. The first thing presented was a picture of a fantastically large cigar-shaped spaceship. It was much bigger than any cruise ship I had ever seen. The trip consisted of a tour of our solar system. The craft was loaded with people that had been picked up at designated 'depots' from each of the ocean cultures. On the dome of each 'depot,' was a hieroglyph symbol that resembled a Humpback Whale breaching with just the tip of its tail still in the water.

It wasn't hard to connect the hieroglyph with the actual space ship because the 3-D image of that huge space craft slicing the surface of the ocean at about a forty-five degree angle was breathtaking. I was spellbound as the craft left Earth and our moon before orbiting Venus. When the other passengers saw Venus, some of them wondered if their home planed looked like this when their ancestors departed. Others mentioned that Venus and Hell must be sister planets because Venus was so hot and turbulent. The ship zipped by Mercury before it shot through an arch formed by a solar flare and jumped into deep space. The narrator explained the next planet reached was Pluto, its moon Charon and even the two mini moons Nix and Hydra. (I didn't even know Pluto had a moon let alone two other satellites) The pictures were unbelievable, Pluto and its moons were a lot smaller than Mercury, and in fact the two mini moons looked more like big rocks than moons. The rest of the program was even more fantastic, the ship actually flew through four rings of Neptune and around the rings of Uranus. The program highlighted Jupiter because it was so huge and it has over fifty moons. The two moons that were talked about most were Europa, because it looked like a fluid filled ice ball and Io, because its volcanoes were in a constant state of erupting. If I had to pick a favorite planet, it would be Saturn (after Earth of course) because it was so mysterious with a hexagonal shaped formation at its North Pole (which had clouds running around it like race cars on a racetrack) and the South Pole looked like a big donut, (with a very deep hole) but was probably a huge hurricane of some kind. The tour ended with cruising by the two moons of Mars before landing on the Red Planet. (It was the only planet the crew felt was safe enough to get a ground-level view. The ship didn't stay long and as we headed back to our "blue marble" planet, the narrator informed the passengers they had been in the vicinity of almost 150 moons in our solar system. I was so enthralled with their presentation I completely lost track of time. Just before falling asleep, it dawned on me there were no commercials in the whole program. That is what I call great TV

Chapter 5

Sacha

My sleep phase was interrupted by a knock on the door. Groggily I forced myself awake with, "Come in." Raising my arm slowly I forced my eyes open and learned it was only 6:07. With that bit of information my head sank back into the pillow and my arm fell across my chest. A second louder knock rousted me out of my slumber. With my eyes closed, I reached for the remote. Grasping it I started pushing buttons with my eyes still only half open. First the shower door opened then the door to the commode opened and finally the TV came on and a voice asked if I wanted something to eat. I started swearing and yelled, "**COME IN !**" as I finally reached a sitting position. To my surprise, standing in my room was the blonde from behind the desk at the Sports Complex. We each were caught just starring at the other for a few seconds until the TV asked again if I was ready to order. She spoke first by asking if she should come back later when I've dressed.

"No!" I stammered, "I'll just throw on a robe and be right with you."

She laughed and as she handed me my robe and noted room service was still waiting to see if I want anything to eat. Diving into the robe, I woke up enough to ask her if she was hungry too. She informed me she had already eaten, so I told room service I was not hungry at this time but thanks for asking.

I apologized for my swearing and bedeviled appearance. She apologized for staring back but this was the first time she had seen anyone with hair on their chest.

"What is this fascination with hair?" I asked. Then I told her the story of the little boy and the people I'd seen giving me quick stares.

"I can see where that would be confusing. Hair is not common here."

"What do you mean? You have beautiful hair."

"Thank you but this hair was implanted."

"You could have fooled me, why did you do that?"

"Because my brother contacted me and said a friend told him there is an opening to work at the San Diego Zoo in two of your months. Without hair I'd stand out like a sore thumb, it's in our genetics, none of us grow hair. In fact almost all the people here that have hair have spent time on the surface with you dry-landers."

"Oh darn! So it was my chest hair, I thought when you came in you were impressed with my manly physique."

"I'm afraid not, I have two older brothers and they ran around our house in shorts most of the time. Just a couple generations ago we thought people with hair were inferior. It wasn't until we got to know you that we were positive."

"WHAT?"

"I was just joking. We realize we are a lot alike since humans came here for tours. In fact there are some things you are better at than we are."

"Like what?"

"Let's not get into that now. I want to finish the story about our changing views on hair. Hair has evolved into a status symbol now; only people who have completed our higher education phases get to have hair implanted on their body. One of the signs of an Educational Professor is to have hair implanted on his or her head. If they are outstanding in their field, they can have hair on their face. When I saw hair not only on your head and face but on your chest as well I was shocked. No one I know is **that** important!" (I was still having trouble getting the picture of a female professor sporting a beard out of my mind) After a recovery pause, I continued:

"I probably do look a little ragged, I didn't even bring a shaver with me."

"We don't have much use for shavers here; anyway, you'll do my image good just being seen with such a hairy man . . . Just kidding."

"Back at ya, but I'm not kidding."

"Did I insult you?"

"No, I just gave you a compliment. By the way, we have been talking for while and I haven't even asked for your name, will you tell me what it is?"

"I would but I don't have one. Here we don't need names because we have been taught how to focus our telepathic abilities in order to isolate the person or group we want to communicate with. My parents don't want me to pick one. They said if I do, they don't want to hear it or have me use it around them. They are afraid if we keep selecting names, that will encourage everyone to talk out loud like my generation does, and then we will lose our telepathic ability. I keep telling them times are changing and we can handle both but they don't agree. The fact is we find ourselves talking out loud because it's fun and maybe it's just wanting to being a little defiant."

"That's interesting. I doubt if I'd ever understand 'silent talking' anyway."

"Silent talking? That's one way of describing it."

"Since you are going top-side, have you decided on a dry-lander name yet?"

"Not yet but I have been working hard to come up with one. Do you have any ideas? You must know a lot of people."

"I know a few but picking a name is serious business for us dry-landers."

"I've searched some of your books on picking names and have found it is a lot harder than I thought. I have picked a few. Do you want to see?"

"Okay, let me take a look."

Her few names took two full printed pages. We decided the best way to come up with a name for her was to go through the list and draw a line through the ones we liked the least and repeat that process until we ended up with at most ten names. Then we would look up the derivation of each of those names and see which one best fit her personality. According to my watch, we spent at least ten hours before we decided on 'Sacha' because it meant 'defender of mankind' and she figured it fit her goal in life. The more we said SAW SHA, the better we liked it. We said the name so many times it almost became a chant. All of a sudden she jumped up, threw her arms around me, gave me a big hug which knocked me off balance making me stumble, fall back and sit on her bed. Then she put her hands on my cheeks and gave me a big kiss right in the middle of my forehead.

I have to admit I was a little stunned by her action but tried to regain my composure by saying, "Is that what you call a kiss?"

"Yes, yes, yes," she replied as she kept on dancing in circles. Then continued, "I feel like a great weight has just been lifted off my shoulders!"

She was so exhilarated I didn't want to bring her down but I had to remind her the application needed a middle and last name also. Sacha stopped dancing and looked at me like I was crazy, "Three names? I need three names?" I explained almost every dry-lander had three names.

"I don't believe you."

"Show me the application and I'll prove it to you."

"You know? . . . I think I remember seeing three spaces for my name. Will you help me fill it out?"

"I can help you with your name, but that's all. You will have to complete the resume yourself."

"I know, but I would like you to read it over in case I misinterpret some of their questions."

"Sounds good, where is it?"

"It is in my apartment, do you want me to go get it or shall we work on it over there?"

"I don't know about you, but I'm a little hungry. Why don't we eat here first and then go to your place?"

"I have a better idea, I know a great little café on the way to my place that has great food." Then a cute little smile started spreading across her face and she added, "That way I could show you off to my friends."

"Oh, you want me to go bare-chested?"

"I don't think so." she replied. With that, I started for the door, but she stopped me with, "Wait! You might as well pick up those shorts in the corner and I'll show you where they belong." We were almost to the stairs when she pointed to a rectangular clear window in the wall and said, "There, put your shorts in there." As I reached for the window, it opened and I completed the task.

Walking down the stairs, I made a comment about none of the doors in the building having locks. Surely there is someone in the building that feels unsafe.

Cocking her head slightly with a quizzical look on her face she simply said, "Why?"

I fired back, "You can't tell me you don't have burglars, rapists or murderers in a city this large." By this time we had reached the outside door and were walking down the street.

"Crime is so low here, we only have four constables, two for the sleep phase and two while the rest of us are awake. The constables are highly trained in thought pattern detection and if anyone even thinks of hurting someone, a lot of people will know about it and the constables are alerted. We don't have to worry about thieves. Everything is free already. Murders! I can't remember even one. Rapes? Sex is such a low priority here, if anyone ever contemplated rape, they couldn't possibly keep it to themselves."

"What if the constables abuse their power and use a person's thoughts against them?"

"I don't know how that would happen when so many people have the same ability and training."

We reached the café and were seated before she asked if there was any thing special I wanted. I reminded her, she had picked this place and bragged about how good the food was, so I'll let you order for both of us.

The waitress hurried over to our table and said, "Hi Sacha!"

"How . . ." then I remembered this "tele" thing and didn't finish the sentence. Sacha thanked her for calling her by her new name and then the waitress just walked away.

"What just happened here?" I asked.

Sacha told me my dinner would be a surprise. She hoped I would like it. We made small talk for a while and then the meal came. After we had eaten she asked me if I liked it.

"The meal was delicious" I responded. "What was it?"

"Are you sure you want to know?" she asked.

"If it's that bad, maybe you could tell me later." I recanted.

"Suit yourself." With that, we got up from the table, thanked the waitress and I started reaching for my wallet.

"What are you doing?"

"I know you don't have to pay for meals but I was just going to leave the waitress a tip."

"That would be an insult to her. It's like you are saying the meal is as worthless as your money. Besides what would she do with a ten-dollar bill anyway? Hang it on her wall?"

"Thanks for the tip, looks like I only open my mouth to change feet."

"What?"

"Never mind, Sacha!"

It was only a short distance before we reached her apartment. Sacha lived on the bottom floor of her apartment building and from the outside, it looked a lot like mine.

As we entered her room I noticed it was quite a bit different though. For example, she had carpet on the floor; her bathroom was a room in itself with a regular door, not a sliding door. She not only had everything I had in my room but she also had her TV situated so she could watch it while lying on her bed, sitting in her big stuffed lounge chair or sitting at her desk. I asked if I could try out her lounge chair and she nodded yes. As I was getting comfortable in the chair she was retrieving the work application from a machine that looked like a small TV with a partial typewriter keyboard in front of it.

"What is that?" I queered.

"My AIO computer." She replied.

I noticed her computer would light up when she spoke to it and go blank when she spoke to it again. "What does a computer do?" I questioned.

"What do you mean?"

"Is it a tool or a toy?"

"It's a tool for gathering information and is programmed to react only to my voice."

"Can you print the information you gather with it?"

"Certainly, that's how I got this list of names. It can do a lot more than print, that's why they call it an All-In-One computer, pointing to some symbols across the top of the keyboard." She no sooner finished her sentence when she began to laugh out loud, "I'm sorry, I forgot you can't read." And then she laughed again and threw up her arms and pleaded, "You know what I mean."

A moment later her mood changed. With a slightly dejected look on her face she came over and sat on the arm of the chair and said, "If we had that much trouble with the first name, how long is it going to take for the other two?"

I looked up at her and explained that normally only one of the three names was used to denote something the parents felt was important and the other two names could be linked together so the names flowed off your tongue. In other words, to make the person's complete name easy to say.

"Can you give me an example?"

"Like, uh . . . Sacha Marie Roberts. See how easy that is to say!"

"Do you know someone with that name?"

"No, that was just an example that I felt flowed off my tongue."

"I like it, is it okay if I use it?"

"I don't see why not."

"Wait, isn't your name Roberts? I believe your guide mentioned it to me."

"Yes but that doesn't make any difference, there are a lot of Roberts in the San Diego phone book. I'm sure even if there is another Sacha, chances are her middle name isn't Marie."

"Okay, I'll put Sacha Marie Roberts on the paper. Now that that is taken care of, I'm curious as to what your three names are."

"Me? I'm Michael Eugene Roberts but my friends call me Mike."

"Hi! Michael Eugene Roberts, my name is Sacha Marie Roberts. What a coincidence. Thanks for helping me, I'll see if I can finish this application now."

She didn't ask any more questions and fell into her resume. I fell asleep in her chair. I don't know how long I was asleep but when she finished her work, she woke me. I must have slept pretty hard because it took me a second or two to realize where I was. I looked at my watch and it said 7:35, the problem was I wasn't sure if it was morning or evening. These continuous lights have messed me up. I thought I'd be a little clever so I asked if it was close to her sleep phase and she replied that she wasn't tired yet.

That didn't help so I asked, "Is it AM or PM?"

As soon as I said it, I knew that was another stupid question and of course she replied, "We don't have AM or PM, in fact have you even seen a clock since you arrived?"

"Of course not." I replied, and then continued, "I think I'll return to my apartment and get a little more sleep. Will I see you tomorrow?" She affirmed she would be by after her sleep phase and would use this time to plan something different for us to do. The walk back to my apartment was uneventful; I flopped on the bed and quickly continued my sleep.

Waking, my watch said it was 5:15. Starting to push the 'window' button I stopped because I knew it would be light out side so I took a shower and this time did everything right. I was even amazed how efficient blow-drying was. Getting dressed and then sitting on the bed I decided to watch a little TV. The first thing to come on was a sports show. It took quite a while before I realized they had teams that used the facilities down at the Sports Complex to play all kinds of different sports and they had play offs and the whole nine yards. Maybe that's why I didn't see many fat people here. I had a hard time turning off the 3-D-TV but I was starting to get hungry again so instead of having food brought to the room, I decided to visit the café Sacha and I ate at earlier.

After depositing my used clothes in the rectangular window, I headed out of the building and walked into the café. Hardly anyone was in there but the new waitress on duty now was not as eager to take my order as the other one was when Sacha was here. Maybe it was just my imagination but I felt she was trying to ignore me. I was a little apprehensive to say anything because I'd almost insulted them last time by trying to do something I thought was appropriate. After about fifteen minutes I was almost ready to take my robe off and show them my hairy chest. I bet that would get their attention. Letting that thought die of its own accord, she finally came over to my table and said, "Are you the one who was here with Sacha?" I was almost afraid to admit that I'm the guy, but I answered, "Yes." I thought to myself, that's pretty good. Sacha picks a name one day and everybody knows it the next day. Then the term 'day' made me realize I would never get used to their 'phases'. As soon as I answered, her whole attitude changed and she became very pleasant. I decided to use this opportunity to find out what was so delicious yesterday so I asked her. Her face went blank for a moment or two and then replied that our waitress told her we had Octopus, seaweed salad and Beluga Whale's milk. No wonder she didn't want to tell me. I thanked her for the information before I asked for waffles with an egg on top and a cup of coffee. Before the waitress walked away, she informed me Sacha was on her way and would be here shortly, did I want to wait for her? Instinctively, I turned toward the door to look but turned back around and settled down facing the opposite direction.

A short time passed before Sacha entered and sat with me. While eating breakfast I asked if she knew my guide well enough to tell him how sorry I felt for his loss. I saw how shook-up he was hearing of his grandfather's death. She told me he was very close to his grandfather and their family was very closely knit. Only the inner circle of family members could attend the funeral. As far as knowing him, he was younger than her and in a different set of educational phases. Though she didn't see him very often she still considered him a good friend almost like a brother.

Since I had no way of contacting him, I asked her if she would give hem my condolences. She agreed to do it the next time he contacted her. She went on to explain that it is impolite to contact someone you know during his mourning period.

"I take it you're my guide now."

"That's right, I'll be your guide until your assigned one returns."

"Can we just sit here and talk for a while?"

"Sure, what do you want to talk about?"

"First, since I know your name now, what is the name of my guide?"

"He doesn't have a name yet. Only people who work top-side get names. Names are like hair, they are only status symbols. They are nice at first but if you don't wear them properly, they can become a detriment."

"Okay, that makes sense. The next thing is, I want to know more about you."

"Really? Well that won't take very long. Where do you want me to start?"

"Why don't you start with when you decided you wanted to work in the environmental field and continue right up to today?"

"Wow, it is hard to remember when I didn't want to improve the quality of our oceans. I do know the exact moment I dedicated my life to Marine Biology."

"Tell me about it, I've never had an epiphany."

"It occurred when my parents, two brothers and myself were on a short holiday trip cruising near the edge of a submerged cliff that dropped vertically to one of the deepest parts of the Atlantic Ocean. We had encountered a large school of Onion-eyed Grenadier and I was commenting on how they looked like swimming daggers when our ship was hit from behind by a deep-sea drag net. My dad had to use all his skill to get us untangled before the net damaged our vessel by dragging it across the ocean floor. I remember being very afraid and my father being very angry. He wanted to ram and sink the trawler pulling the net but my mother calmed him down a little and we shot through the surface a short distance off the trawler's bow and flew straight home. I don't think my father ever got over that experience. He still wants to sink every deep-sea trawler that lays miles of drift net killing many species of fish that the fishermen just dump overboard. A good thing did come out of it though, my oldest brother became a Marine Biologists and the other teaches Oceanography in Southern California."

"I understand why that experience would encourage you to be involved with Marine Biology but wouldn't it be great if you worked at the San Diego Zoo? You probably know I am from San Diego." (Why I added that last part was a mystery to me.)

For the next dozen or so time phases, Sacha and I visited many interesting places. Like the time we toured a power station. She took a saucer shaped vehicle this time, slipped out the underwater exit tunnel and skimmed along the bottom of the ocean for quite a while before coming to a forest of hydro-thermal vents. She stopped, sat the craft on the bottom and we began to sink slowly down a shaft only to come to rest in some kind of airlock. The water receded and a big door opened for us to enter. Inside there were many odd shaped machines and as soon as we reached the main floor a young man came over quickly to greet us. I loved the expression on Sacha's face when she heard how he greeted us, "Welcome Mr. & Mrs. Roberts to our facility." I shrugged my shoulders and looked at her and then the poor young man's face turned beet-red and he apologized for his mistake. He told us he was sorry but the noise of the machinery must have prevented him from clearly getting her message. He rebounded quickly and started telling us his machines were an essential part of the success for all the cultures because here they separated the compounds found in sea water into Nitrates and Phosphorus for farming, Hydrogen for fuel, Oxygen and Nitrogen for pure air and most of the Silicon for building purposes. Then he held up a small silver dollar sized wafer, looked at me and said, "Thanks for finding the conversion program disc, it will make processing compounds faster and more efficient."

Most of the places we visited after that were connected with saving the coral reefs or declining numbers in certain fish species. We even visited a station that is working on removing the Mercury levels in fish. The facility she seemed to find most interesting was one working on the problem of harmful algae blooms increasing in size and number all over the planet. She was talking about interrupting the life cycle of the algae somewhere between the cysts germinating and gametes forming into zygotes. I got lost on the cysts but she apparently found it quite interesting.

The trip I found most interesting was the Continental Shelf trip down to the canyons of the abyss. We were so deep the sunlight couldn't penetrate and I experienced many unbelievable sights. She turned the lights off in the craft and we just floated, suspended in total darkness when all of a sudden a bright blue flash caught my attention, then another one; pretty soon they were all around us. She told me what they were but I can't remember what she called them. I think she said they were some kind of shrimp.

After she turned on the external lights, we began moving and I saw the most frightening small fish I have ever seen. It looked like it only had a mouth and tail, the mouth was full of large fang-like teeth and it had a little lantern on its head that glowed. But my all time favorite was the Dumbo Octopus. It resembled the Disney character Dumbo's head with four or five trunks. Where the baby elephant's ears are located, this creature had wings or fins that looked like Dumbo's ears. (and it flapped them in order to swim through the water). There were tube worms, white crabs, snake-like creatures with big heads and so many different forms of life down there it would be impossible to describe all of them.

The most unusual feature of the ocean floor wasn't the abyss (that she said could hold Mt. Everest with room to spare) but a circular patch on the floor of the Gulf of Mexico that looked like a lake. Around the "lake" was a heavy population of clams, shrimp and worms. There was nothing growing in the interior of the circle. Sacha said, "Watch this!" and she set our submersible down hard in the center of the 'lake' and concentric rings of waves fled away from us. She did it two or three more times and we had made waves under the sea. She told me the pool was just a high concentration of salt, then mentioned there were rivers and even waterfalls down here also.

Finally the day came when she told me my first guide was coming back to work and she was about to start her job at the zoo. I had gained a lot of respect for Sacha and her passion for trying to solve problems involving the sea.

I knew I had deeper feelings for her than she did for me but I thought I'd give it one more try before we separated so I asked her if we could celebrate when we got back to my apartment. She agreed to come over after she cleaned up and had something to eat. I interrupted her and suggested we have dinner at my place and explained the food was great. To my surprise, she accepted as our craft settled into a docking slip. She must have 'called ahead' because there was a "bubble car" waiting to take us home.

I wanted that night to be special so after I 'spruced-up' a bit, I had a talk with the TV waiter/cook explaining this was a special meal for two and I would appreciate it if he would surprise us with a meal he deemed appropriate. He looked back at me and said, "No one, as long as he has worked with dry-lander visitors, had asked him to be creative." He thanked me and concluded with, "I'll do my best."

I didn't have to wait long before hearing a knock on the door. Standing in my doorway was Sacha in a conservative dress, hair down over her shoulders and a pair of slingback sandals.

Before I could say anything she twirled around making her dress billow-out and said, "How do you like my new work clothes?"

All I could think to say was, "I'd hire you in a second!" I could tell she was in a good mood by the way she sashayed over to the foot of the bed and sat down.

A second knock at the door revealed the waiter pushing a little cart which had a silver plated bucket full of ice, a bottle of champagne chilling and two crystal Champagne glasses. While he was pouring the wine, Sacha stood up and walked toward the table. The waiter excused himself and then announced that our meal would be here in a little while.

Sacha gave me a curious look and asked, "Just what are you up to?" I answered with, "Just a little celebration for you and your new job." I don't think she bought that but she didn't push the issue. I decided to lead the conversation in a different direction so I asked, "What do your parents think about your new job?"

"Oh, they support me in anything I decide to do."

"That's nice, I thought your dad wasn't too fond of dry-landers." I noticed her glass was losing Champagne a little faster when I mentioned her father.

"He is fine with it. He just thought I'd work in one or our facilities."

Her glass was now empty for the second time so I refilled it for her. Before the next question could be asked, the waiter was at the door again. This time the linen-covered cart contained two covered plates; the waiter set Sacha's plate on the table and then ceremoniously removed the silver cover to expose an artful display of calamari, two anchovy fillets with parsley and lemon wedges. I believe he called it Calamari Ripieni, which he topped off with a bottle of white wine complete with a crystal wine glass. My plate contained a two-inch thick Filet Mignon cooked medium rare with a twice-baked potato and a helping of fresh white corn topped with a melting butter patty. Next he completed my setting with a matching wine glass and a bottle of red wine.

Seeing this fantastic food, I stood up and shook his hand telling him he had outdone my wildest expectations. Before he left he said he would pick up the dishes in the morning, smiled and made his exit.

I think Sacha was impressed too because she became very quiet, almost to the point of being subdued. She just looked at her food until I asked her if she wanted to trade meals.

She raised her eyes till they met mine and exclaimed," No, of course not. This is the most perfect meal I have ever seen. Thank you, I have never been emotional over a meal before." I didn't want to burst her bubble by telling her who had really planned the meal, so I simply said, "You're welcome." We didn't talk much through the meal or a couple more glasses of wine, but we were both a little less inhibited than ever before. I asked her to tell me something about herself that she wanted to tell me but hasn't yet." I knew what I wanted her to say and could tell the wine was starting to take effect but I was completely unprepared for her answer.

"Something I haven't told you huh? . . . I have never told you I am a Christian, that I believe Jesus is the Son of God. He came to Earth to save our souls, He was resurrected on the third day and will appear to us on Judgment Day just like God did on our home planet."

That was not what I expected but this woman rarely did or said anything I expected. I told her that I believed the same thing but was still surprised at her answer because her people had been around thousands of years before Jesus was born.

She looked me as straight in the eye as she could and stated, "We believe God sent Jesus to save us too, God has always wanted people to worship only Him and live according to His teachings. Jesus is the only person who spent His life doing both, so He has to be the Son of God. Besides, in the Book of Mark, Jesus told His disciples to "go ye into all the world and preach the gospel to every *creature*." We know He didn't mean ordinary animals when he said creatures, we feel He was including us."

After a while I asked, "Why do you think God sent your people to Earth instead of just taking them to Heaven with the rest?" She thought for while, then answered, "I hope it is for what we are trying to accomplish here but to tell the truth, I have no idea; I don't try to get into the head of God. His reasoning is far above my comprehension." "The only way I can explain, to my own satisfaction, why God does what He does, especially why He lets people be killed; whether in wars, hurricanes, tsunamis or any other natural disaster, is to believe He put us here to test our resolve as to whether or not we truly believe and trust in Him. I have witnessed many incidents where I thought God was punishing me, only to find out later that what I thought was a punishment turned out to be a blessing in disguise. We should be prepared all the time because the final test can come at any moment."

I was shocked at her Christian commitment so I asked if the reason she believed in Jesus was because He was one of them?

With a questioning look on her face she informed me Jesus was just what He said He was, the Son of God and Man. She continued, "I believe in God's love for us because I can't think of a more profound way to prove pure love than to let your only child die a horrible death on a cross just to pay for the sins of everyone, even the people who tortured Him like that. The deciding factor was when Jesus proved He demonstrated His power over death by rising from the dead, talking to people who knew him before He died and even eating with them. No ghost I've ever heard of eats or drinks with his friends."

Then she started telling me stories about Jesus as a little boy and some of the miracles He performed. Like the time Jesus and a friend were playing on a roof of a shed and both boys fell off with His friend breaking an arm. The boy began crying loudly and Jesus came to him and put His hand on the friend's arm and it was mended with no pain instantly. Or the time they were playing by the town's water well and a little girl who was sitting on its edge, fell in. Jesus looked down at her and told her to "rise", she floated in air to the top of the well where He slipped His hands under her armpits and set her feet on the ground. Some of the children told their parents but nobody believed them. There were many more stories that weren't in our Bible that she relayed to me in great detail.

I asked her how she knew these stories and she replied they were first-hand written accounts that had been handed down generation after generation by her people.

The more she talked the more she drank until at one point she extended her arms toward me, stood up, took a few steps and sat on my lap with her arms hanging around my neck. With a slight slur in her voice, she whispered, "I like you."

Now I knew she was drunk, way too drunk to walk home by herself so I said, "Do you want . . ." That's as far as I got because her forehead nuzzled on my neck and her body went limp. She was asleep. No way could I carry her home so I picked her up, carried her over to my bed and tucked her in for the night after slipping off her shoes. I was feeling the effect of the grapes also but realized that bed was not built for double occupancy. Walking back to the table I decided it would be a shame to let the rest of the wine go to waste so I sipped on it as I watched her sleep. She looked like a cherub after a hard day playing. A wicked thought of taking advantage of her in her condition did cross my mind but she looked so peaceful and pure, that thought turned rancid even in my impaired mind. I knew I wanted her but only of her own free will, not like this. Finally I finished the rest of the wine, put my feet on the other chair and fell asleep knowing Sacha was very important to me.

I woke up still sitting in the chair, my head was pounding, my mouth felt like I'd been grazing on cow-pies, and when I looked in the mirror I quickly closed my eyes before I bled to death. Slowly I surveyed the room to find Sacha gone and the plates missing. I must have slept like a rock because I could swear I had a mouthful of dirt. I wasn't completely alone though; there was a note from Sacha on the bed. It said, "Thank you for everything; hope to see you again top-side." I needed a handful of Aspirin but settled for a cold shower, tried to brush the mud out of my mouth and combed my hair along with my scrawny beard. I put on a clean robe and was ready for the guide to arrive.

Chapter 6

Tour Ends

I almost fell asleep again before he showed-up. The first thing I did was to offer him my condolences for his loss.

With his head bent slightly he said, "Thank you, my grandfather was the most loving man I knew. He is the reason I decided to become a Communicator. When I was young, I would sit through full wake phases while he told me exciting stories of the battles he fought in during the war."

"Which war?"

"The Revolutionary War."

"You have to be kidding, It is hard for me to believe you talked to someone that had to be close to 250 years old."

"I don't lie. One of the stories he told me most often was when he fought in the Battle of Cowpens. My grandfather was a sharpshooter under General Morgan. He told me the general originated the saying, "Don't shoot until you see the whites of their eyes!" He also developed the tactic of shoot three times then retreat to your second line of defense so they could fire three times while you were reloading. This would continue until you sucked in the enemy to where you could outflank them resulting in their capture.' He believed that military strength and preparedness were extremely important for humans but good communicators were essential for peace.

"I loved listening to his stories of triumph. The thing he impressed on my mind was that war was a very ugly business and should be abolished if possible." He always emphasized the main purpose of a Communicator is to prevent war. First by finding common ground in a dispute, then expand those areas by communicating an understanding between the two or more adversaries."

"That sounds good but we haven't had much success in that area."

"My relatives relayed to me that before my grandfather died he told them that he was very proud of me and I had a crucial opportunity to help save Earth."

"What do you think he meant by that?"

"I know exactly what he meant but we will get into that if I am successful." "First I want to thank you for being a gentleman to Sacha. You proved you were the man we were looking for just as our emissary said you were."

I felt a little betrayed by Sacha telling anyone about our last meal together. To me it was a tender moment that didn't need to be shared with anyone else. "Exactly what did she say?" I blurted out.

"That's what she said; That you were a gentleman. Was there more to tell?"

"Not exactly." If that's all she said maybe she thought it was special too. Anyway, it did feel good to finally be able to say 'not exactly' to him for a change.

"I think there is one more institution I should show you before your tour is complete."

"I've seen so much down here, I can't think of anything else to cover."

"According to the itinerary, you haven't seen our medical facilities."

"You're right. A city this size must need a medical center if only for people getting injured while participating in activities at the Sports Complex."

My guide retorted with. "This is a full functioning hospital, we are very proud of our doctors, staff and life-saving equipment."

As we drove to the only hospital for the whole city, I asked him if this trip would be uncomfortable for him since his grandfather just died here? He informed me his grandfather died in his home with his wife by his side. Only after he passed did she inform the rest of the family. "That's the way it is done here." he added.

"I'm interested in the funeral if it's not too personal or painful to talk about."

"Why would it be painful? He lived a very rewarding life, we think he accomplished every goal he set out to achieve. It was his decision to let Nature take its course. He believed that if you believe and are faithful to your Creator, God lets you know death is near before you complete the act of dying. We believe at the moment of death, the soul leaves the body and enters a spiritual dimension which can't be seen by mortals but its presence may be felt. It is in this spiritual existence, we join your relatives while ascending to be with God until the soul and body are reunited on Judgment Day. Our custom is to place the shell (or body) of our loved one in a torpedo shaped black coffin before we accompany it in a hearse shuttle. The shuttle takes the coffin and family members into space. The funeral is complete when the family is through reminiscing and the shuttle's torpedo tube propels the coffin toward home in the direction of Orion's Belt.

That was a little more than I wanted to hear but by this time we had reached the hospital and parked into another soup bowl.

As we toured the hospital it was apparent not very many people got sick here. I counted two people with their head wrapped in a shiny material that looked a lot like tin foil. One other person with what looked like welder's goggles covering his eyes, lying on a bed being bathed in a very strong light and the last person was on a gurney being guided down the hall.

"Not a very busy place, is it?"

"That's the way we like it and there are many good reasons. I believe the most important reason is preparation."

"How do you prepare to go to the hospital?"

"Maybe preventive maintenance would be a better term. At birth we extract a person's nucleic acid to get their genetic blueprint so we can keep them healthy. That's why we harvest Stem Cells from the mother's placenta for every baby born here, making sure they are kept viable the entire life of the individual. With that information we can reproduce any organ or gland in the body; we can surgically remove a malfunctioning part and replace it with a healthy one grown from the person's own DNA. That eliminates rejection. I believe people on the surface take the baby's hand and foot prints but we take eye scans also for identification and everything goes into our data bank." He continued, "Another reason the hospital is prepared to treat any individual instantly upon arriving, is because the blanket you sleep under each night is imbedded with sensors set to the parameters of your particular medical biorhythms. If the sensors pick up a reading outside those parameters, a signal alerts the hospital and an ambulance is dispatched.

I was going to ask him what nucleic acid was but I was afraid he would tell me.

The whole idea of having that much information on me or anyone else seemed to infringe on my right to privacy, but privacy was almost nonexistent down here anyway. I'm sure that was important to him but it was getting close to lunch time for me, so I was happy when we had completed the hospital tour and hopefully finished the last item on the itinerary.

He drove to the same place we had eaten before but his time when we entered the restaurant I ordered a hamburger, French fries and a strawberry milk shake. My guide gave me a quick look and then with a smile more than a smirk, just shook his head and said, "I'll take the same thing, except make mine chocolate."

My next question was, "How much of your food do you get from us dry-landers?"

"Not very much, most of the produce we get from our hydroponic farms and almost all the beef, pork, lamb and chicken we eat comes from our ranches and farms.

"You own cattle ranches?"

"Of course some of our ranches are still on dry land but we have domed ranches on the ocean floor camouflaged with a stealth material to look like the surrounding area."

"You're kidding!"

"Not at all, after the dome is anchored and all the water is pumped out, we install lights that mimic the Sun's light, grow grass, pipe in fresh air and water then raise all kinds of animals. In fact our largest ranch covers over ten thousand acres."

"That's impossible, one of our submarines would have spotted something that large or at least heard noise from the animals."

"I have to admit you have come close to finding a ranch or two but our sound buffers are triggered by sensors placed in strategic spots just for that purpose. "We have had one slip-up when a submariner hydrophone operator heard a rooster crow and wrote it down only to have one of his superiors talk him out of leaving it in the official record."

"You wet-landers seem to be awful lucky when it comes to us dry-landers reporting your existence."

"I think knowing 'human nature' is a lot closer to the truth than luck.'

"What do you mean by 'knowing human nature'?

"We know when and where to let you see us so it won't be reported, or if it is, it won't be believed."

"Give me an example!"

"Okay, the best example of knowing human nature that comes to mind is the crew of Apollo 11. When they were on route to the Moon we let the astronauts see us as we scanned the capsule to make sure everything was working properly. We found a few problems and fixed them with a diagnostic ray. We were worried they would see flashes of the ray because it's frequency is very close to visible light. To tell the truth, we didn't believe you had the computer power to get into Space let alone land on the Moon and return to Earth safely."

"I never heard anything like that! They would have said something."

"It did happen and that's what I mean about human nature. Humans make choices based on what is most important to them at the time. If they would have said anything, they knew that landing on the Moon would be scrubbed and they would have had to return to Earth for psychiatric evaluation."

"Even if that is true, I still think you are lucky."

"Luck has very little to do with it. We have been with you since before your written history began and we know where to place our people to maximize our security and minimize any serious reporting you may have attempted."

"I thought the main reason you brought me here was to let me report what I see?" "That's now . . . not earlier."

"What's so special now?"

"I'll give you four reasons: First, have you noticed how your knowledge of science has exploded in the last forty years? That is **not** by accident, you have come close to discovering us so many times it won't be long before we can't deny our existence any longer and we need you to be ready. Second, you have polluted the planet to the point that a climate change is going to occur in order for the Earth to stabilize itself again. Third, The proliferation of atomic weapons is at a point where it is just a matter of time before someone starts an atomic holocaust that will leave the Earth uninhabitable and that means the oceans too. Fourth, but not least, we need your help because we have tracked an asteroid for about five years and it looks like it may barely miss Earth in April of your year 2029 but returns in 2036 and has a higher probability of colliding with us somewhere in the Pacific Ocean. The odd thing about the pass-by and possible collision is that they both occur on a day you have demonized as unlucky for years; Friday the 13th."

"You're kidding, right?"

"No, I'm not. But I do find it ironic that you have deemed Friday the 13th as unlucky and now you will have a very good reason to perpetuate that superstition."

"Is the asteroid large enough to wipe us out like the one that killed the dinosaurs?"

"No, this one is about a half-mile in circumference. I'm told it would fit snuggly into the Rose Bowl Stadium at Pasadena."

"Don't you have the technology to divert the asteroid?"

"We haven't tried, it is so large and unstable that if we push too hard it will break-up and we would have thousands of smaller impacts hitting the Earth destroying a larger area. Since your scientists will know of it in the near future, we are worried you may try to explode a nuclear devise on or near it and that would be disastrous because not only would you be bombarded with hundreds or even thousands of meteorites but they would be radioactive too."

"Do you have a plan to save Earth?"

"Yes, but we need your help. We have to let all the humans on Earth know our story, and that we are not invaders like most people think. That is where you come in. You must write a story telling people what you have seen here and try to calm their fears before we make ourselves known to everyone. Once we have that cleared, we will be able to help your culture get up to speed."

"What do you mean, get up to speed?"

"There is going to be spillage no matter how we eliminate the asteroid threat; Our plan is to let the asteroid pass Earth the first time and when it gets to its apogee, we will try pushing it into Venus' gravitational field so it can't return. If that doesn't work and it breaks-up, like we think it will, there will be more pieces returning than we can destroy. That's where we have to get you up to speed so you can destroy the ones that get through us. We will destroy as many possible in deep space and you are going to have to clean-up the rest."

"I see the urgency now, I think it's about time I return home."

"We agree. Make sure you tell your culture we are your friends, we are not here to invade. We live with you on the same planet and want to protect it as much as you do."

"Good, this has been a very interesting stay and your advertisement was true."

"Advertisement?"

"Yes, one of your emissaries told me this would be a story I would tell my grandchildren, and hopefully he will be right."

"Okay then, I'll have someone pick you up at your room about twelve o'clock according to your watch. Will that be sufficient time for you to get ready for your trip home?"

"That will be plenty of time, it's only four o'clock now. That gives me eight hours."

"I'd stay with you but I have to prepare for our next visitor. We think we can squeeze one more in. We are running very short on time."

"Will you answer two unrelated questions before you go?"

"If they have short answers, what are they?"

"Why does everyone here wear white robes, when I saw with my own two eyes, your factories make all kinds of clothing?"

"I thought you would have figured that one out. We believe everyone has different abilities and skills but no matter how smart, good looking or talented you are, you are no better or worse than anyone else. In order to remind us of that fact, we decided many generations ago to wear these robes. What is your second question?"

"I could have sworn the other night when I was watching television, I could smell appropriate odors that went along with the 3-D pictures. Was I just imagining that?

"Not exactly. (I hope that is the last time I hear that phrase.) The reason you experienced a particular odor was because of subliminal messages projected on the screen. They make your subconscious mind think you smell what ever they want you to smell. If those are all your questions, I'll send a taxi to pick you up."

"Oh! I just remembered something else that I wanted to ask."

"Ok, but I'm starting to run late."

"When I arrived, there were two other people with me, why didn't I see them again?"

"One of them decided to stay here and go through the education phases. The other one didn't stay very long, she proved to be untrustworthy."

"Untrust . . . ."

"That would take to long to explain I really have to leave now. Bye!"

"Alright, thanks for everything. I am sure I can find something to do." In my mind I thought, 'like look-up Sacha and say good-bye.

I didn't go straight back to my room. A taxi pulled up and I had him drop me off at the Sports Complex. I entered the building quickly, expecting to see Sacha behind the desk, but she wasn't there. A redheaded woman behind the desk told me Sacha left for her job at the zoo right after lunch. Then she added, "Aren't you the guy . . . . " I stopped her by nodding my head up and down, turned around and left the building. Now what was I going to do? I just stood there for a while before deciding to go back and apologize. I told the receptionist I was sorry for being rude, that there was no excuse for it. She seemed to accept the apology so I told her I had over seven hours to kill before I left for San Diego. There was a lull in the conversation before she suggested I try one of the sports-programs.

"Name something you are interested in." (I almost said Sahca but didn't.)

"When I was a youngster, I saw a news-reel about a P-51 Mustang pilot shooting-up German trains and getting into dog-fights but as I grew older that didn't sound as much fun anymore."

"Do you want me to try finding a program like that?"

"Why not!" She looked for quite a while before she punched out a card.

"I think this is close to what you are looking for." She handed me a card and I thanked her before walking down the hall looking for an empty room. Finding one, I inserted the card and had no idea what the menu said. Luckily the receptionist was standing behind me because she figured I'd have problems. We decided to start with an easy program called "Bridges & Trains." I thanked her and when the door closed behind me, I was in a classic flight suit and about to enter a P-51 Mustang with three other Mustangs ready to go with me.

The sound was deafening as two of the planes pulled out onto the runway and then I pulled out with the third plane. All four of us revved our engines until I thought they were going to break apart, eased off on then and brought them back to a fever pitch as we eased off the brakes and picked up speed down the runway. I seemed to jump off the ground with the throbbing Rolls-Royce Merlin engine pushing me back in my seat as we climbed to twenty thousand feet. I was starting to feel comfortable in the cockpit when a voice came over the intercom, "Follow me!"

I felt the plane's nose rise and then roll over in a bank to the left and all four of us lined up in a dive at a narrow bridge over a deep canyon. As we picked up speed I could see the anti aircraft shells exploding around me and feel my blood racing through my veins. The plane shook as we reached four hundred mph. Out in front of me I could see the lead plane release a thousand pound bomb that hit a gun emplacement on the left hand side of the canyon. That silenced it. The other side of the canyon was still firing as the second P-51 tried to hit the bridge but missed and the bomb exploded in the river beyond. The third plane got hit and began spiraling toward the earth. I couldn't see if a parachute opened but after I released my bomb a big hole in the bridge opened up with chunks of the bridge falling to the river below.

The other two pilots started cheering and congratulating me as we climbed out of danger. Our leader told us we were deep in enemy territory and to look for targets of opportunity but to make sure we had enough fuel to get back to base. He peeled off with his wingman which left me alone.

Still having one bomb and full magazines of 50 cal ammunition, I was starting to enjoy how responsive the aircraft was when little flashes of light began streaking by me. I dropped my right wing and started to dive. It wasn't until then I saw a train with flatcars spitting bullets at me that I pulled up and made a wide circle out of range of the tracers buzzing as they passed. With a few adjustments, I gained a little more altitude, inverted that Mustang, started my dive and gave it full throttle before lining up my gun sights with the railroad tracks. The guns on my wings started pounding 50 cal lead balls back at them until about the third car I stitched exploded into a fireball that almost knocked me out of the sky. I pulled back on the stick as hard as I could until the nose pointed skyward. Next I pulled hard to my left so I wouldn't play tag with the mountain coming up fast. Missing the mountain, I gave the Mustang its head until the altimeter revealed she had galloped to over thirty thousand feet. That's when I started leveling out and taking a second look. A tunnel a few miles ahead of the derailed train fit the description of a target of opportunity. I have a bomb left, and that would be a good place to deposit it. Circling the train I lined up the tracks again. Going into a strafing dive I pumped holes in the train again all the way through the engine before I let the bomb go free. I must have been lucky on the bridge because all I did was dig a hole in the tracks a hundred yards from the tunnel entrance.

The fuel gage indicated it was time to go home and it was so real I felt compelled to return to base. Soon I landed and the program ended with me sitting on a chair in an empty room. The first thing that went through my head was, "I just gotta get one of these things." I almost decided to go out in the hall and do it over again but this time picking an advanced program.

A glance at my watch said it was a little after nine o'clock so I returned the card to the desk and started a conversation with the redheaded receptionist. I asked her how well she knew Sacha. She replied that Sacha was her best friend and they grew-up together.

"I don't know how to put this but did she say anything about me?"

"Of course! She described you to a tee."

In a flippant manner, I said, "In order to describe me, all she would have to say is 'a guy with a scraggly beard.' Guys walking around here that have beards are about as rare as hens' teeth."

The redhead gave me a puzzled look for a few moments and then said, "hens' teeth? I'll have to remember that one. I think she likes you because she said you are nice and a gentleman. Then she said something a little odd, 'I may make this name permanent'."

"That's all? Is that good or bad?"

"Well, it ain't all bad."

"All right! I'll ask. Do you think I have a chance with her being more than just a friend?"

"That, you will have to ask her yourself."

"Well, thanks anyway. I'll try looking her up when I get home." With that I left the Complex and headed back to the apartment.

In my room I found my shirt, shorts, pants, shoes and socks all arranged neatly on the bed so I got cleaned up and dressed in my regular clothes. I still had over two hours to go before twelve o'clock. For some reason I wasn't hungry or thirsty but I pushed the 'food' button anyway. Luckily the friendly face appeared once more. He started his usual question when I interrupted him and said, "I'm fine, I just wanted to thank you again for that fabulous meal and table setting last night, I mean, pre sleep phase." He got a big smile on his face and replied, "Thank you, good luck with your story and God be with you." With that, the screen went blank and I was all alone again. I might as well relax on the bed, but before I do, I'm going to take that blanket off.

I woke up with two well-dressed gentlemen standing at the foot of the bed. "Time to go" one of them said as he held out his upturned hand.

"What do you want?"

The well-dressed gentleman replied: "Your communicator please."

When we left, instead of walking to the front door we walked up the stairs to the roof. (I thought: Why don't they have an elevator in this building?) On the roof, a triangular craft had the hatch open. We climbed aboard and the craft hovered for a moment before heading for the bay. Once there it knifed through the water and out the exit tunnel. A short time later we slipped through the surface of the Pacific Ocean and flew toward the darkened coast of California. Moments later we were landing next to a paved highway where I was instructed to walk to the car waiting on the road. I hadn't taken more than five steps when I turned to see the triangular craft lift off and disappear into the night. I wanted to return to the spot occupied by the craft but I knew I would find three evenly spaced indentations where the landing pods were. I approached the car and it was the same powder blue Cadillac that had taken me to the yacht.

Chapter 7

Back Home

I was a little apprehensive as I arrived home. The car simply stopped in front of my building, let me get out, and then drove off rounding a corner never to be seen again. Nothing looked like it had changed, so I tried my key in the foyer door and it worked. I walked by my mailbox and it was empty as usual, even my room looked like I just walked out the door. I don't know what I was expecting. Everything was the same but different. I sat in my old chair, turned on the old TV and watched part of an old movie I'd seen before. Nothing was the same, maybe I was bored or it was just a let-down from the excitement I had just experienced. Anyway, I was tired and got ready to retire, turned off the lights and TV before climbing into bed. It felt very good to be in my own bed, knowing it didn't have any sensors sewn into the blankets and the best thing of all was that it was dark outside my window.

The next morning I decided to call work just to see if I still had a job. The store manager answered by saying his name and of course his title. When I identified myself and asked when I should start work, he informed me I had been replaced by another "Butcher Boy," but I could pick up my last paycheck in his office. While I was gone my rent had come due and I didn't have any money so I'd probably be thrown out of my apartment too.

That thought had barely cleared my mind when there was a knock on my door. When I opened it the landlord thanked me and asked if I had a good trip. Before I could ask him why he was thanking me, he said he appreciated being paid for last month and this month in advance and if there was anything he could do for me just let him know. As I was closing the door I could have sworn he bowed a little bit. This guy looked like my landlord but the only way he would be so nice was if he thought I came into a lot of money.

I was just too physically and emotionally drained to look for a job today so I wandered over to my refrigerator and automatically opened it. I must have stood there for thirty seconds or more before realizing I was gazing into an empty box. There must be some kind of magnetism in a refrigerator because this was not the first time I found myself standing in front of an open refrigerator with no reason; I do it almost every time I visit my parents. It was depressing to see nothing in the icebox but there was a letter on the kitchen counter from my father so I sat down and began reading it. Mainly, he was asking if I was planning a trip home anytime soon. After reading the letter, I went to the cupboard and opened the door. I jumped backwards when a can of soup fell out hitting the counter before bouncing onto the floor. Looking in the cupboard revealed it was full of canned fruit and vegetables, snacks, and my favorite brand of peanut butter. Before I could pick up the soup can, there was a knock on my door. Standing in the doorway was a teenager with a cardboard box on a hand truck. He asked my name and I told him. He trucked the box into my room and asked me to sign a sheet on his clip-board.

I asked him, "What is this all about?"

He said, "I don't know mister, but this box is cold and heavy and it is yours whether you sign or not." Before I could ask another question, he left the box, took his hand truck and closed the door behind him. Cold and Heavy? What would be cold and heavy? I had to open it, so I took out my knife and cut the tape around the edges. To my surprise, the box contained packages of meat wrapped in butcher paper with labels like, Rib Steak, T-Bone Steak, Hamburger, Sausage, and many others. There was enough meat to last me quite a while so I put some in the fridge and the rest in the freezer. Someone was making sure I could "hole-up" for a while and I was starting to wonder why.

I started checking out the room more thoroughly only to find the one thing out of place was my camera. I remembered I had placed it on the shelf but instead of the camera, its open case was there instead. Checking to see if the camera was in the case, I discovered ten one-hundred dollar bills and a note. The note read: "Use this money to pay for your necessities while you write your story. When you finish, send the story to the address on the attached card." I held the card and looked at it in disbelief,. $1000 for a story! I didn't know if I should feel honored or bought. Well, I figured if they were going to pay, I'll write the story. But before I start, I will find out just where I stand with Sacha.

It didn't take as long as I thought to contact her. I did have one interesting conversation with a person at the Conservation and Research for Endangered Species facility in San Pasqual Valley. I was asking if they had a Sacha Roberts working there and she said she would check. Coming back on line she informed me she couldn't give out that information. I told her my name and she asked if I was her brother. I knew then I was on the right track so I lied and told her I was her oldest brother. That seemed to do the trick. She informed me Sacha had been sent to them but they didn't need her full time so they sent her to the Wild Animals Park that was just down the road. I thanked her and asked if it would be possible to get their number. After thanking her again, I dialed the number she gave me and asked to speak with Sacha Roberts. The woman wasn't familiar with the name and asked if I was sure she worked there.

"Only recently," was my response.

"Oh! The new blonde girl, yes, but she is out in the field right now, can I leave her a message?"

"Fine, will you tell her to call Michael Roberts when she has time?" After giving her my phone number, she agreed to give Sacha the message and we hung up.

The longer I waited by the phone, the more nervous I became until finally I put things in perspective by asking myself why was I obsessing about this girl? I had to tell my fellow dry-landers that the people they have been calling Aliens all their lives are really our brothers and sisters from a destroyed planet. It seemed ridiculous to be nervous about a phone call.

It was a good thing I went to my typewriter and started writing the story because she didn't call until about ten o'clock that Friday night. I was taking a break by looking out the window just before she called, thinking how great it was to actually experience darkness again. I don't think I will ever take nighttime for granted again.

It was great to hear her voice again; I could feel the tension ebb as she told me about her job with the baby elephant and lion cubs. She was so excited even if it wasn't the job she had been trained to do. She continued by telling how different it was to actually touch these animals and she went on and on. Finally I got a word in edge-wise and told her I wanted to see her, not just talk to her. She quieted down when I said that, and then explained her next day off wouldn't be until next Wednesday.

I got a feeling she was surprised when I said, "Fine, I'll see you on Wednesday." There was a little silence, and then I added, "Where are you living?"

She gave me her address and phone number and said she got off work about six-thirty. Shortly after telling me that, she yawned softly before hinting she was really exhausted and needed to get some sleep.

Not really the phone conversation I had hoped for but I was sure it would be different next Wednesday when we met face to face. I had a lot to do before next Wednesday, so I dove right into my story. I think I wrote and rewrote the story at least ten times, but by Tuesday it still didn't quite sound right. I ended up leaving the part about my feelings for Sacha out because that was none of anyone else's business. I put the story in a manila envelope and mailed it off just as I had been instructed.

Wednesday morning I got up early, called Sunset Inn where she was living and rented a room for tonight. My next project was to procure a car that would impress Sacha. It was about time I got rid of that old Studebaker anyway so I drove it down to a used car lot where my eyes almost popped out of my head as I spotted a beautiful dark blue 1970 Dodge Challenger. I didn't get a very good deal (I think showing the salesman five crisp one-hundred dollar bills tipped him off I was eager to buy that car.) but I did become the new owner of a car I couldn't afford. Anyway, I figured Sacha was at least two hours away so I had to leave by noon in order to make sure I got there by the time she got off work. I hoped she would recognize me with a haircut and without my beard. After showering and shining my shoes, I dressed in my best everyday clothes, packed my best (only) suit in the suitcase and headed downstairs to the parking area where my "Trophy Car" was waiting.

It was 12:07 when I pulled out of the apartment building's parking lot and headed for Escondido. The Sun was bright, the sky was a beautiful blue and it was just a great day for traveling. Studying the maps for the last few days had paid off, I had no trouble finding the motel and where Sacha worked. In fact she was still working when I saw her for the first time in over a week. She was a little embarrassed because I found her cleaning out a cage, but she seemed excited to see me and that was a plus. She was impressed that I had a car because she was forced to ride the bus every day. I told her I had just bought the car and I lost my job. (Two dumb things to put together when you are trying to impress someone, and by the look on her face I knew I didn't impress her in the least.) Then, trying to salvage some dignity, I continued, "but I got some money for writing the story so I'm okay."

"OH! You've written the story already?"

"Yes, I had a lot of incentive to complete it by today."

"I'm glad you completed your task."

"How about I take you out to dinner?"

Sacha smiled, "That sounds good to me, I need to go back to the Inn and clean up first."

"I think I know the way, if I make a wrong turn just let me know."

We got in the car, drove straight to the motel, got dressed and before long were walking into a nice restaurant with candles on each of the tables and soft music floating in the air. I was in my suit and she was in a cocktail dress that revealed a little more than I wanted other men to see. After we were seated and ordered, I complimented her on her dress, all the while trying to concentrate on her face.

She noticed my straying eyes by rearranging her dress before saying, "Now you know why we wear robes." I could feel my face getting hot so I know I must have been blushing. "I'm sorry, I didn't mean to stare but you are more beautiful tonight than I thought possible."

"I really don't understand why a woman's mammary tissue gets men so excited."

I was acting like a kid with his hand caught in a cookie jar so I tried to act more manly by saying, "I could tell you but I'd rather show you."

"Oh? I think we had better change the subject." she suggested. I was all for that, I'd run out of smart-ass quips anyway. I asked her how she ended up working with lions and elephants instead of whales or algae. She had just about finished telling me how she messed up the first interview when our meal arrived.

After the meal I picked up the check and left a tip on the table. She looked at me and then the tip and I could tell what was going through her mind.

"We are in my culture now." I said. She knew what I meant and let me help her with her shawl before we stopped at the main desk to pay.

In the car, I asked her if there was any place special she wanted to go. She suggested we just relax and drive around taking in the sights. She had been there only a few days and didn't know the area. We drove for about an hour before she commented on how different I looked without a beard. She thought I looked a lot younger and thinner than she remembered.

I wanted to tell her again how perfect she looked but instead, I told her, "You clean-up pretty good yourself." We laughed about the night we got drunk on the wine and I told her how I wanted to take advantage of her, but didn't. She confessed she was not as drunk as she pretended. I didn't know how to react to that information so I started telling her about flying the P-51 Mustang. She commented that she had never used that program.

Finally we decided to go back to the Inn. I suggested we get a couple of bottles of wine on the way home but she said no, she has done that before and doesn't want to do it again. I finally talked her into one bottle of Merlot. It wasn't long before we were in my room and I was opening the bottle while she was taking the paper off two plastic glasses. I made the comment that these crystal glasses looked a lot different that the ones before. She acknowledged my attempt at a joke with a soft little giggle as she set the glasses down to be filled.

We sat at the table just like before but about half way through the bottle, I could tell a mood change by her facial expression. I asked her what the problem was as I noticed a tear form in the corner of her eye. I extended my arms in an attempt to console her and she laid her hands on my arms to stop them.

She raised her head with tears slipping down her cheeks and said, "I love you."

I thought my heart was going to jump through my chest. "I love you too, more than you can know!" I exclaimed.

"No, you don't understand." She continued. "We can't be together. We can never see each other again."

"Why? I don't understand? We can work this out." I stammered.

She calmed down a little and the tears started to dry up when she added, "We can't be together because I am already married."

I know my lower jaw must have bounced off the table and my heart slipped all the way to the soles of my feet before I could form the words, "What? When? And Why?"

Her composure was coming back now and she said, "You forgot Who?" I almost laughed but how do you laugh with a broken heart?" I felt like the world stopped and I fell off, just tumbling through endless space. The long silence was finally broken with,

"I've been married to your guide for about forty of your years. Our parents arranged our marriage when we were very young. The ceremony was performed when he entered his educational phase, but we will not live together until we decide to have a child."

I was stunned, but finally I countered, "How can a society as advanced as yours have such primitive customs? Forty years, did you say forty years?"

"Yes, forty of your years, she answered. "You were told we have longer life spans than you."

"But you look like you are in your early twenties now. Just how old are you?"

"Where we live I am still a young woman, you know we don't measure time in years."

"I don't care about your age, I love you now and I always will."

"Michael, you know in your heart it can't be, I love you too, but I love my family, their honor and our culture more. Besides, the timing is not right. Neither of us are ready for a committed relationship."

"I wish you would have told me this right from the start."

"Now, I do too. I was flattered that a dry-lander could make me feel the way you did. I didn't fall in love with you until after that last fantastic meal we had together. I knew you had more plans for me that night than just the meal. I think part of me was expecting to be ravished by a sex crazy dry-lander that I had heard so much about, but I didn't fall in love with that man at the table, I fell in love with the gentle man that slept in his chair. I know I would have regretted that time if it had turned out any differently."

"Sacha, I have mixed feelings about that night. One minute I'm proud of myself, the next I'm thinking what a fool I was to let an opportunity to show you how much I cared, escape."

"You are not a fool, you learned, and you taught me a very important lesson."

"What? You can fall for a fool and I can fall for a married woman?"

"Of course not, we both learned we have the ability to love. There are few people who **have** had the wonderful feelings we experienced."

I wasn't sure I bought that last statement but what choice did I have. After an uncomfortable pause I answered, "I guess this is good-bye, I'll be heading home tomorrow, but I'll never forget you."

"I will never forget you either, in fact when my husband graduates and has to pick a name to work top-side, I'm going to try talking him into choosing Michael."

"Why?" I asked.

"I already love a Mike; I think it would be easier to transfer that love to him if I didn't have to change his name."

"I must be crazy, but I almost feel flattered. The only trouble is, another Sacha will be a lot harder to find." We both got a little laugh out of that ironic thought. Finally I regained enough strength to stand. Putting both my hands on either side of her face, I gave her a kiss in the middle of her forehead.

I knew as she walked out of my room, she was walking out of my life also. When the door closed, I started to feel like my life was closing too, but the next morning I had my first epiphany. I clearly understood that this experience of love with Sacha had changed me from a "Butcher Boy" into a man. Now I could get on with the rest of my life. It's been a long time since I've seen my mom and dad. I think that would be a good place to think things over. That said, I'd never forget my first true love.

Epilog

The year was 2007, the time was after 5:00 p.m. and the place was Las Vegas. If not for a chance meeting, this story would be complete. My wife, Barbara, and I were playing poker machines at Texas Station in northern Las Vegas when a woman bent over and asked if the seat next to me was taken. I responded automatically with a "No, you can sit there" as I glanced up at her. That glance sent my mind reeling into overdrive. I knew that young woman but couldn't place where I knew her from. I just sat there looking at my machine until I felt a touch on my arm. The woman looked at me and asked, "Is your name Michael?"

"Sacha!" I exclaimed, "It is you!" (My wife turned toward me so fast she almost fell out of her chair. I don't think she ever really believed me when I told her of my trip under the sea.) As the shock subsided, Sacha introduced us to her husband Anthony Turner. (At once I remembered her telling me she would try to get her husband to pick the name, Michael. Apparently that didn't happen.) He reached to shake hands and said, "Hi Mike, nice to see you again." I introduced my wife Barbara and we all just stood there speechless for a few seconds. Finally Tony suggested we all go have a drink together in the casino's bar.

It amused me that Barbara made sure she sat between Sacha and me at the table. Even after twenty-seven years of marriage, I could see a little speck of green in Barb's beautiful blue eyes. One other thing I noticed was, this was the first time Barb ever left a machine that she hadn't cashed-out.

As we settled into small talk, I commented on how young both of them looked. I said they looked young enough to be our children instead of being old enough to be are parents. Sacha smiled and stated that they didn't feel they were quite that old. We conversed about our families, jobs and special interests," A short pause ensued before Anthony commented, "What a small world this is, what are the odds of us meeting here in Vegas?"

"Not very high," I agreed.

"How is your gambling going?"

"About the same as usual. We arrive, we donate, and we go home."

"I agree, personally I don't like to gamble but Sach does. I enjoy the shows the most."

"Barb is the one in our family that likes to hear the bells go off and the money drop into the bins. She keeps telling me she is going to hit a big jackpot some day. I just hope I'm around to see it."

It was inevitable that our conversation migrated to that month I spent with them over thirty years ago.

"Mike, it's good to see you again, I know I don't have to pretend I don't know you like I have to do to so many of the others that visited us. Our life up here isn't exactly what we had in mind because we have had to pack up our belongings and move across the country many times just to get away from some of the other Americans I've guided.

"Americans, don't you mean "dry-landers?"

Tony almost broke into a laugh, "Boy, it has been a long time since I've heard that term. We have called you Americans, Europeans or Asians depending on what part of the world you come from for a long time now."

"Did you ever get to work in your field as a Communicator?" I asked.

"I did for a little while until one of our "visitors" recognized me and threatened to expose me as an alien. His extortion attempt ended my usefulness so we moved and had to find new job.

Tony got a little more serious look on his face when he explained the program in which I participated was abandoned shortly after my departure. When asked why, he explained that only a small percentage of the people wrote the report as I did and that most of them used what they saw to "invent" products that were technologically too advanced for human society to use properly.

He continued, "The Information Council decided we didn't need your help with the Friday-the-thirteenth asteroid. We are confident it will not collide with the Earth. The council figured if we gave you the technology to change the course of near-earth asteroids, you would probably end up destroying Earth just like we destroyed Kaylig, our home planet."

Then I asked, "Tony, is there anything new about the Friday-the-Thirteenth Asteroid?"

"Your scientist named it 'Apophis' and it is going to come closer to Earth than we first calculated. Now we think it may take out one or two of your satellites as it passes by."

"What if you're wrong and it hits Earth?"

"Let's hope we are not wrong. However, the worst case scenario says it would have an impact equal to 400 megatons of TNT. To put that in perspective, you've heard of the Krakatoa eruption? Well it was calculated as a 200 megaton explosion."

Sacha ended the conversation with, "That's enough serious talk, I need to go to the powder room. Barbara, do you want to come?" Barb jumped at the opportunity and they both disappeared around the end of the bar.

Anthony began telling me about how the Culture Council may decide to change their territorial plans after the threat of the asteroid has passed. He told me they may be going back to their home planet Kaylig if possible.

"I thought you said Kaylig had been destroyed completely in a ball of fire!"

"That's what we are going to find out. We have sent a Galaxy Class Cargo Ship toward the three stars that make up Orian's Belt so they can determine if it's inhabitable again after all the generations we've spent here"

"If it took you fourteen generations to get here, how can you get back so fast?"

"We have had a break-through in space travel recently."

"Break-through? Can you tell me about it?'

"Sure, it was weird how it came about though."

"Now that you have peaked my curiosity, please continue telling me about it."

"Okay! We have been working on a faster method of transportation for a very long time. Then one day during a lunch break, an Oceanic Geological Research scientist, who had been working on tsunami's unusually high speed through the deep ocean, was communicating with a Deep Space Propulsion specialist. The geologist was explaining to the specialist how a tsunami triggered the incredible speed obtained. All of a sudden the Space Propulsion specialist's face froze in a weird expression just before he jumped into the air as he yelled, "I've got it!" That outburst resulted in a lot of lunch trays being spilled by a startled group of workmen.

The propulsion specialist went on to say, "I know how to create a space tsunami, all we have to do is fold the Dark Matter in space by compressing it in front of our ship and letting it expand behind us. When that fold builds up enough pressure and snaps, it will trigger a wave we can ride like a surfboard that will be faster than the speed of light. All we had to do is learn how to turn and stop it, then we can go anywhere.

"You are going to fold Dark Matter?" I asked, then I continued asking, "I've never even hear of Dark Matter, what is it?"

"To tell you the truth, I don't understand either but this is what they told me. It is invisible matter that holds galaxies together and over 90% of the Universe is made up of it and Dark Energy."

"How did they come up with that?"

"We learned the speed of the stars in each galaxy,(except the ones being drawn into the Black Hole) travel at the same rate. That was odd because we felt the stars farther away should travel at a reduced speed as it does in this solar system. The speed of the planets are regulated by centrifugal force and the gravitational pull of the Sun. Since gravity between two objects loses its power at the rate of the distance squared.

The only thing that could possibly explain stars keeping their same rate at the edges of a galaxy as they do near the center, is there must be some type of matter holding the galaxy together. We also concluded there had to be an energy supporting the matter so we called them Dark Matter & Energy."

"I guess that's reasonable, but how does that tie in with a tsunami?"

"I'll try to explain it like this."

Tony picked-up a cocktail napkin and drew a dot at the top and another one at the bottom, labeled one 'start' and the other one 'destination', as he forced the two dots closer together the napkin folded in the middle. "In space we can do basically the same thing by compressing space in front of our ship and expanding it behind us. However, as we compress space in order to bring our destination closer, there is a limit to how much it will 'fold' before it triggers a tsunami type wave which carries us on its crest. The refinement of locating this trigger point has allowed us to cross great distances in short periods of time. The big advantage is since the ship is controlling the rate of speed at which space is being manipulated, we can accelerate and stop in space by regulating the rate of compression and expansion with no ill effects on our crew." He continued, "An over simplification of the idea is like a surfer catching a wave, the surfer looks like he is going fast and he covers a long distance, the reality is that the wave is actually doing the moving. The surfer is just along for the ride." He concluded, "The most difficult problem we had to overcome was not starting or stopping the wave, but vectoring it to go where we wanted."

"So is that what people have seen when they reported seeing a UFO dart across the sky and make sharp turns that seemed impossible?"

"What they probably saw was some unmanned flights where we were testing mutable vectoring techniques. We have been working on the Spatial Fold Theory for over thirty of your years and have just perfected it recently. Now that we have the ability to travel distances measured in light years, the Council figured it was time to leave."

When God told us to be caretakers of Earth until you were able to take over, the cultures agreed that this new ability could be a sign telling us the covenant has been fulfilled. We could finally stop hiding from you and reclaim our home planet.

"Wow! are all your cultures going?" I questioned.

"Yes, all five cultures worked to perfect this theory and we all feel it is time to leave. If our ship finds Kaylig has rejuvenated itself, the crew will contact us and we will begin the exodus home. We pray God will give us a second chance to inhabit our planet. If He doesn't let us live on Kaylig, maybe He will let us find a uninhabited planet we can call home."

"It's going to be strange for us humans not to have UFO sightings anymore."

"I wouldn't count on that, most of the reported sightings in the past were explainable through natural phenomenon, or your military experimental aircraft. You will probably be sighting many more encounters after we're gone."

We just sat there sipping our drinks when I noticed a familiar smile/smirk spread across his face before he said, "Mike, Sacha told me about your infatuation with her and I have to admit I was a little jealous for a while but after thinking about it, I came to the conclusion you did me a favor."

"That was a long time ago but how do you figure that?"

"Here's how I see it, Sacha is a great person and even if I wasn't her first love, it made me realize I had a rare woman with the capacity and ability to love. That made me work a little harder to earn her affection, that, in turn, made me fall more deeply in love with her and for a man and woman to love each other where we come from is very rare. Our culture treats love more like an obligation than the beautiful emotion it is.

Tony saw the girls coming so he changed the subject by asking me if I was still in the meat cutting business. I responded, "Not exactly." (We just sat there silently staring at each other until finally both of us had to laugh at that response)

Barbara and Sacha joined us and asked what was so funny? Tony and I looked at each other and he replied, "Oh nothing, just something that happened many years ago."

I could tell that Barb was a lot more comfortable with Sacha now, than when they walked off to the powder room. I was curious what was said to make such a difference so I asked, "What did you girls talk about?"

Barb answered with, "Oh, just something that happened many years ago." The women laughed.

Before we parted, Tony shook my hand and stated, "You Are Us as we were many generations ago, learn from our mistakes."

Sacha slipped Barbara a small circular disk with some numbers on it and told her if she ever wanted to visit, all she had to do was follow the instructions they talked about. We waved good-bye and they were swallowed up by the crowd.

I turned to Barbara and asked what Sacha meant about visiting. Barb just gave me a mysterious smile and replied, "What do you think she meant?"

So, if you ever see three circular shaped indentions in our lawn and we are not anywhere to be found, we have probably been whisked away by a UFO.

The End

CPSIA information can be obtained
at www.ICGtesting.com
Printed in the USA
FSHW02n0929070818
51136FS